Carry On Abroad

The wickedly funny story that starts where the film ends

Norman Giller

Chameleon

For George, Alan and Kenneth
The Best of Brothers

First published in Great Britain in 1996 by
Chameleon Books
106 Great Russell Street
London WC1B 3LJ

CIP data for this title is available
from the British Library

ISBN 0 233 99031 3

Typeset by Falcon Oast Graphic Art

Printed in Great Britain by WBC, Bridgend

Author's Acknowledgements

This book could not have been written without the original foundation work of *Carry On* film creators Peter Rogers and Gerald Thomas. I have simply carried on where they left off, but I would not even have managed the first step without their marathon screen productions to inspire me. I am also indebted to the *Carry On* team of actors, who brought their characters to life on screen and turned the film series into a national institution. I acknowledge, too, the lovingly crafted screenplays of the writers, and in particular Talbot Rothwell and Norman Hudis. On behalf of the Publishers, I thank the Rank Organisation for allowing us to step into the *Carry On* territory that has always been exclusive to the silver screen, and for their permission to use still photographs from the original film version of *Carry On Abroad.*

My thanks also to VCI Chief Executive Steve Ayres for letting me off the leash, and to Tim Forrester, Tom Rosenthal and John Cleary at Chameleon Books for their encouragement; also to my House Editor Stephanie Goodwin, and to Richard Percy, who first had the brainwave to turn the *Carry On* films into books. Most of all, thanks to Eileenalanna, Lisa and Michael for being there.

The characters and events depicted on the following pages are entirely fictitious, and anybody who wishes to argue otherwise will be laughed out of court. *Carry On Laughing...*

Introduction

This book carries on where the film *Carry On Abroad** left off. The story so far:

Stuart Farquhar (Kenneth Williams) is a courier with Wundatours, a dubious take-the-money-and-run travel company that specialises in cheap and cheerful package holidays to the Mediterranean resort of Elsbels. This is in the 1970s when the package holiday craze is at its height and standards are at their lowest. Thousands of British tourists, many of them on their first trip abroad, are herded around the Costa Packet like cattle, and among them is a coachload of tourists under the care of the fairly eccentric and totally inefficient Farquhar.

They are booked into their still-being-built hotel to find a few minor problems, such as no hot water, windows without glass, exploding electrics, food that you would not feed to your dog and the little matter of a missing roof. The hotel is very loosely run by warring husband-and-wife team Pepe and Floella Ripoffola (Peter Butterworth and Hattie Jacques), with the help of a staff

*The classic comedy film *Carry On Abroad* is available in the *Carry On* series on Cinema Club videos, distributed by VCI, price £4.99.

of just one: Giorgio (Ray Brooks), a waiter more interested in laying the guests than the tables.

Our story starts at the beginning of the following tourist season, with reluctant courier Stuart Farquhar about to welcome another party of jolly holidaymakers on behalf of Wundatours. Bookmaker Sydney Roper (Sidney James) is there and, unfortunately for him, so too is his put-upon wife Ethel (looking for all the world like Joan Sims). Sydney had been hoping for a solo holiday so that he could continue his long-running affair with Sadie Tompkins (a Barbara Windsor lookalike), who always has a couple of points to make and is on the look out for husband number three.

The always-complaining Blunts, Stanley and Evelyn (Kenneth Connor and June Whitfield) have turned up to throw a shadow on all around them. The Golightly sisters, identical twins Gladys and Gladys (both portrayed by a Patsy Rowlands lookalike) are on board hoping for some slap and tickle at the double, which smooth Scot Bertie MacConway (Jimmy Logan) will be happy to provide. Martha Arkwright (Patricia Hayes) is making her first flight, along with her dead quiet husband Percy. 'The Very Reverend' Francis Bigger (Frankie Howerd), undertakers Ivor Bodie (Terry Scott) and Bernie Biddle (Bernard Bresslaw) and private detective James Bedsop (Charles Hawtrey) are also part of the package. But they are not on holiday. They are each on special assignments.

Waiting to welcome them to Elsbels in their new, almost-finished hotel are Pepe and Floella Ripoffola, with their over-sexed, underpaid conniving head waiter Giorgio. They have many extra surprises in store for their guests – in the form of many extras.

On with the sun-cream, the shades and the kiss-me-quick sombrero... and *Carry On reading*...

1

LUTON AIRPORT, WEDNESDAY 30 MAY 1973

Two o'clock in the morning and Stuart Farquhar was stationed at the Wundatours check-in desk with a fixed grin on his face and a sinking feeling in his stomach. The fact that he was standing here at the start of a new tourist season wearing his sickly salmon-pink company blazer with a huge 'W' on his breast pocket represented the biggest defeat of his life.

He had vowed at the end of the previous season that he would never again allow himself to be subjected to the degradation of courier work. Nursemaid, agony aunt, diplomat, entertainer, shepherd, general dogsbody, translator, purser, bingo caller. These were just a few of the roles he was expected to fill as he faked friendliness and respect for clients he secretly considered cretins. It was all beneath a man who, while at Great Yarmouth University, had got a first in domestic science.

Farquhar widened his grin as he saw the first of his party of fourteen clients approaching. He quoted the company motto, fighting not to vomit the words out: 'Welcome to Wundatours where everything is wonderful and *you* are the most wonderful of all.'

Sydney Roper, in cream lightweight wide-lapelled suit with flared bottoms, red kipper tie and black Cuban-heeled boots, was the first to arrive as a walking advertisement for why the Seventies were considered the height of fashion (apart from by anybody with a modicum of taste). He was followed by his wife, Ethel, wearing a simulated leather skirt and jacket, with shiny, white knee-length PVC boots. On her shoulders she was balancing their mock crocodile-skin suitcase.

'You the geezer in charge?' Sydney asked, wincing as he took a close look at the salmon-pink blazer. 'Blimey, with a jacket like that you must be. You wouldn't wear it unless it was for a bet or you were getting paid. I wonder what the "W" stands for.'

Farquhar wanted to say something about the pot and the kettle, but remembered his company policy: 'The client is always, always right regardless...'

'I'm Stuart Farquhar, and I am the courier who will be seeing to it that you have the holiday of a lifetime,' he said, sticking closely to his company script in a voice that had a peculiar pinch-nosed nasal sound. 'And you are...?'

'Sydney and Ethel Roper,' said Sydney. 'Where can my missus put the suitcase? Bloody heavy, that is.'

Farquhar helped Mrs Roper place the case on the scales. The arrow jumped twenty pounds past the baggage allowance.

'Oh dear,' said Farquhar, 'I'm afraid you have excess baggage.'

'I didn't want to bring the old bag,' Sydney whispered. 'But she insisted. Ruined me 'oliday before it 'ad even started.'

'I 'eard that, Sydney Roper,' his wife said. 'You honestly don't think I'd let you out of my sight for a whole week, do you? I wouldn't trust you to keep that little thing of yours in your trousers for five minutes.'

'I was referring to the luggage, Mr Roper,' Farquhar said, determined to keep out of any domestic squabbles. 'You are twenty pounds over the allowed limit.'

Sydney rounded on his wife. 'I told you not to pack them tins of baked beans,' he said. 'The food in Elsbels has improved out of sight, ain't it, Stu?'

'You have no worries about the food at the hotel where you will be staying for the next seven days,' said Farquhar, crossing his fingers beneath his clipboard. 'It boasts a *cordon bleu* chef, and there will be a full English as well as Spanish menu.'

'See,' said Sydney to his wife. 'I told you we'd get the full Monty for our twenty-nine quid a head. Blimey, that's a month's wages to them dagos.'

While Mrs Roper was unpacking the case and removing ten tins of baked beans and her ironing board, Farquhar was welcoming his next clients. 'Welcome to Wundatours,' he said, 'where everything is wonderful and *you* are the most wonderful of all. I'm Stuart Farquhar, your courier. And you are...'

'We're the Blunts,' said Stanley Blunt, perspiring under the weight of three suitcases and a fully buttoned-up overcoat.

'From Guildford,' said Evelyn Blunt, pulling her heavy tweed coat tighter around her. 'And what we're doing here in the middle of the night in God forsaken Luton I just don't know. We've got colour television and fully automatic up-and-over garage doors. What we're doing going on a tatty holiday like this is quite beyond me. This is for the *hoi polloi* and not what I am accustomed to at all.'

'It's the most convenient time to travel,' said Farquhar, leaning on one of the stock answers in the company's an-answer-for-every-occasion manual. 'There is much more air space, and therefore no annoying flight delays.'

The words were barely out of his mouth when there was an announcement over the tannoy. 'Attention. Flight Number one two six, Wundatours Airlines. The three o'clock departure for Elsbels has been delayed because of a technical problem. Please await a further announcement.'

Farquhar's upside down coat hanger grin widened as he remembered company policy: TURN THE NEGATIVE INTO THE POSITIVE AND MAKE BAD NEWS INTO GOOD NEWS.

'Ah well, more time for duty-free shopping,' he said.

'Listen to me, my man,' said Mrs Blunt. 'My husband and I want no-smoking seats. And remember that we have paid a two pounds surcharge each for a sea view.'

'Everybody will be able to see the sea from the plane, madam,' said Farquhar, his first spontaneous moment of sarcasm that he had vowed to control after being punched on the nose for being too toxic with his tongue at the back-end of the previous tourist season.

'I meant at the hotel,' Mrs Blunt said frostily.

'Ah, of course,' said Farquhar. 'That has all been arranged in advance.' He did not add that she would need a ladder and a good pair of binoculars. He would cross that mountain when he came to it.

'All right, Stanley,' she said, 'don't just stand there. Put those suitcases down, and then go and get me a cup of tea. I'm freezing.'

Stanley was on remote control when in the company

of his wife. After eighteen years of marriage, he had given up making decisions. She treated him like a doormat, and he dreamed of one day pulling it from under her feet. He did what he was told because it meant an easier life. The last time he had stood up for himself, when wanting to watch England play West Germany on television in the 1966 World Cup Final, she had given him the cold-tongue treatment for the following month. The last civil words she had spoken were, 'That ball was *not* over the goal-line.'*

Stanley quietly put it down to her German bias. Her parents were from Koblenz, and Stanley was convinced that she was out of the same line of descent as Himmler.

He had dropped into a dangerous habit lately of thinking what he meant to say and saying what he thought he was thinking.

When instructed to get the tea, he had meant to say, 'Yes, dear.' What he actually said, and which was fortunately unheard by Mrs Blunt, was 'Go and get it yourself, you old crab.'

Farquhar heard it, and silently forecast a major bust-up before the holiday was over. In fact it was a toss up, he thought, as to whether the Ropers or the Blunts would come to blows first. He saw his next two clients approaching. He arranged his face to accommodate the upside down coat hanger smile, even though he thought he was seeing double. 'Welcome to Wundatours,' he said, 'where everything is wonderful and *you* are the

*Geoff Hurst scored a controversial goal for England against West Germany in the 1966 World Cup Final. The ball struck the underside of the bar and bounced down. The Russian linesman decided the ball had crossed the goal-line, but few, if any, Germans agreed.

most wonderful of all. I'm Stuart Farquhar, your courier. And you are...'

'Miss Golightly,' said the first sister.

'Miss Golightly, two,' said the second sister a moment later. She was a full minute younger than her twin sister and that much slower and more immature.

The Golightly sisters were spitting-image twins, so much so that because their mother could not tell them apart she had called them both Gladys. On their birth certificates they were entered as Gladys One and Gladys Two. They thought the same thoughts, and spoke the same sentences. As you would expect, this almost suffocating togetherness had manifested just a little minor psychological malfunctioning which produced just one fairly discernible difference between the sisters. One of them had developed psychopathic tendencies, but which one? Even the twins were not sure. Among the many things the thirty-something sisters shared in common was that they were both man mad, and they had been locked in a race for more then ten years to see who could get to the altar first. As soon as one twin thought she had found her 'Mr Right' he was always frightened away by the other twin. They often raced for the same man, and both instantly zeroed in on Stuart Farquhar.

'Do you come with us...' started Gladys One Golightly.

'To Elsbels?' finished Gladys Two Golightly.

The twins had a disconcerting habit of finishing each other's sentences.

'But of course,' said Farquhar, sensing double

trouble. 'I will be your courier throughout the holiday.'

'What are you...' started Gladys One.

'Doing tonight?' finished Gladys Two.

'Goodness, I have no idea,' said Farquhar. 'I have so much organising to do that it leaves little time for social niceties.'

'We'll soon change...' started Gladys One.

'All that,' finished Gladys Two.

'My, but you are totally identical, aren't you,' said Farquhar. 'How do I tell the difference between you?'

'I'm the noisy, older one,' said Gladys One, loudly.

'And I'm the quiet, younger one,' said Gladys Two, quietly.

'And I've got a blue and red butterfly tattooed on my right buttock...' started Gladys One.

'While I have a red and blue one on my left,' finished Gladys Two.

'I see,' said Farquhar, not seeing. 'Well welcome to the holiday of a lifetime. Please do not hesitate to make contact with me if there is anything you should require.'

'Oh, don't worry...' started Gladys One.

'We'll be making plenty of contact,' finished Gladys Two.

Farquhar was relieved to see his next client approaching. On with the upside down coat hanger smile, and he forced himself not to comment on the sight of a kilt at Luton Airport at two o'clock in the morning. 'Welcome to Wundatours,' he said, 'where everything is wonderful and *you* are the most wonderful of all. I'm Stuart Farquhar, your courier. And you are...'

'Bertie MacConway,' Bertie MacConway said, and

adding loudly for the benefit of the twins, 'My friends call me Big Mac.'

The Golightly sisters were impressed, and now they had another joint target.

'Welcome to the holiday of a lifetime,' said Farquhar, on autopilot. 'Please do not hesitate to make contact with me...'

'Och, away wi' you, mon,' said MacConway. 'This is a mon's kilt I'm wearing, not a skirt. I want nothing tae do with the likes of...'

The words died in his throat as he caught sight of the most ravishing creature ever to come into his view. Porters crashed their trolleys and case-carrying men collided with each other as all eyes turned to drink in the sight of Sadie Tompkins walking towards the check-in desk on leg-elongating platform shoes. Her buttocks, just about covered by the microest of micro mini-skirts, swayed like huge ripe peaches in a tropical wind as she wriggled up to the counter. Two melon-like bulges kept her at arm's length from the checking-in assistant. This was a fruit cocktail for the eyes of the men. The twin sisters, Mrs Blunt and Mrs Roper, particularly Mrs Roper, hated her on sight.

'What the ruddy hell is *she* doing here?' she hissed at her husband.

'Who?' said Sydney, trying to pretend that he was the only red-blooded man in the airport terminal who had not seen her entrance.

'The Trollop,' said Ethel. 'Don't tell me you didn't know she was coming.'

Sydney gave a forced double take as he looked at

Sadie decorating the check-in desk. 'Blimey, Miss Tompkins, what are you doing here?'

'Ooh, 'ello, Mr Roper,' she said, giving an equally bad performance. 'Fancy bumping into you. I'm going to Elsbels for a week. What about you?'

'Well I'll go to the foot of the Himalayas,' said Sydney. 'That's where me and me missus are going, too.'

For Ethel, it was too big a coincidence. It just happened that Sydney employed her as a clerk at his betting shop.

'Are you trying to tell me that you didn't know she was going on the same holiday as us?' she said to her husband, determined not to communicate with or even acknowledge the existence of Sadie.

'Amazing, ain't it,' said Sydney. 'We work not more than a few feet apart...'

'A few inches, I've heard,' said his wife.

'...and here she is catching the same flight as us. Well, what d'you know.'

Ethel knew a lot more than she was letting on, and she had a carefully orchestrated plan to end their little game and to part Sydney 'Know All' Roper from just about every penny he possessed. It was going to be an interesting holiday.

Farquhar greeted Sadie with no need for a fixed smile, although close examination would have shown that his unforced smile was more of a leer. 'Welcome to Wundatours,' he said, 'where everything is wonderful and *you* are the most wonderful of all. I'm Stuart Farquhar, your courier. And you are...'

'Mrs...oops, sorry, *Miss* Tompkins,' she said, not yet out of the habit of calling herself Miss after two marriages that had failed because neither of her husbands could cope with all the attention that she received (and encouraged).

'Ah yes, *Miss* Tompkins,' said Farqhuar, ticking her name on his clipboard. 'Welcome to the holiday of a lifetime. Please do not hesitate to make contact with me if there is anything you should require.'

Sadie weighed him up with an experienced eye, taking in his Mr Punch profile and his flared nostrils. 'Yes, darling, maybe I will, but I 'ope there's better on offer,' she said. 'Now can you point me towards the ladies. I left in such an 'urry that I forgot to put my knickers on. The old welcome mat is frozen.'

Farquhar's face turned the colour of his jacket as he pointed towards the toilets.

Sadie winked at Sydney. 'See you on the plane, Mr Roper,' she said. 'P'raps we can have a highball together.'

All she got from Ethel was a glaring eyeball.

Farquhar did not need to ask who his next client was. The sky-blue cassock, the cardinal's hat and the cross hanging from his neck big enough to hang a coat on. It could only be 'The Very Reverend' Francis Bigger. 'Welcome to Wundatours,' he said, 'where everything is wonderful and *you* are the most wonderful of all. I'm Stuart Farquhar, your courier, Reverend Bigger...'

'*Very* Reverend,' corrected Bigger, as he made a sign of the cross. He handed his case over for weighing, first of all removing a well-used Bible. It was in actual fact a hollowed out drinks container in which he kept his whisky and brandy, purely for medicinal purposes, of course. Under a previous alias, Bigger had been a member of Alcoholics Anonymous, but he had changed his name so that he could start drinking again. He had bought the European franchise to the new Wall Street religious movement, 'the Holier than Thou Church', which had as its main purpose the worship of money. Now he was off to Elsbels to see if he could spread the gospel, despite the stranglehold that the Roman Catholic Church had on that region of the Mediterranean.

He had once spent some time in hospital alongside Sydney Roper, and they knew each other well. His gambling debt at Sydney's betting shop currently stood at three figures.

'Watchyer, Frankie, my son,' said Sydney.

'Hello, my son,' said Bigger, acknowledging him with a sign of the cross that he had been practising hard to turn into the shape of a pound note sign. 'And what brings you wafting into heavenly Luton Airport?'

'Would you believe we're going on 'oliday,' said Sydney. 'I suppose you're taking to the air to try to get closer to your Boss.'

'Verily, verily and thrice verily,' said Bigger, 'I am going to Elsbels to try to ring heaven's bells in the ears of the unconverted. Do you wish to make a donation to help the cause?'

'Do leave off, Frankie,' said Sydney. 'This is Sydney Roper you're talking to. You've got more chance of reaching my soul than my wallet. And my soul, incidentally, begins with an "R".'

Bigger looked at Farquhar. 'How about you, my son,' he said. 'Would you like to make a donation to the

Holier than Thou Church funds?'

'Uh, I'm afraid I'm an agnostic,' said Faquhar.

'But that shouldn't stop you putting your hand in your pocket, my son,' said Bigger, who was equally, if not more, agnostic. He nodded to indicate Roper. 'It's what our bookmaker friend here would call spreading your bet.'

Farquhar lost concentration on what Francis Bigger was saying as his eye was taken by what appeared to be a funeral procession heading for the check-in desk. It *was* a funeral procession.

Funeral director Ivor Bodie, his assistant Bernie Biddle and two airport porters were carrying a coffin at respectful funereal pace to the Wundatours departure point. Walking alone behind the cortège came the bowed figure of a little old lady in widow's black veil and mourning dress.

Farquhar looked wild-eyed down his client list. All he could find was a Mr and Mrs Arkwright. He was too shackled to the company manual to change his script. 'Welcome to Wundatours,' he said, 'where everything is wonderful and *you* are the most wonderful of all. I'm Stuart Farquhar, your courier. And you are...'

Ivor Bodie, who had won the coveted 'Most Mournful' undertaker trophy – a small, silver casket – at the recent Funeral Director of the Year awards, acted as spokesman. 'This,' he said, indicating the coffin as his too-large false teeth made a death rattle sound, 'is the late Percy Arkwright, God rest his soul, and this is his widow, Mrs Martha Arkwright. I am Ivor Bodie, funeral director, and also on the flight with us will be my assistant, Mr Bernard Biddle.'

'But nobody told me that Mr Arkwright was, uh, um, incapacitated,' said Farquhar.

'Well he only snuffed it at the weekend,' said Bodie. 'He and the dear Mrs Arkwright...' He bowed respectfully in her direction, and she gave a half smile from beneath her veil. '...had their hearts set on this holiday. It is their first trip abroad after forty-two years of marriage. Mrs Arkwright knew that Mr Arkwright would want her still to go ahead with the holiday, particularly as your company said they could not refund the deposit. She decided that she would only go if her loved one were to come as well. It has all been passed by your head office.'

Not for the first time, Farquhar found himself oblivious to what was going on inside his own organisation. 'But I'm afraid we could not possibly put him up at the hotel,' he said.

'No worries,' said Bodie. 'We have arranged for him to lie in a Chapel of Rest in Elsbels. The change of scenery will do him the world of good.'

Bernie Biddle, who had won a bronze casket in the Best Supporting Role at the awards ceremony, now had the coffin balanced on his huge shoulders because the two airport porters had gone for their teabreak.

This feat of strength greatly interested the Golightly twins, and each independently decided to also make him a target during the holiday.

'Now that we've checked in,' said Bodie, 'Mr Biddle and I will take the deceased to the aircraft and get him comfortably installed in the hold.'

'Can I come with you?' said Mrs Arkwright, startling everybody around her by suddenly shouting at the top of her voice. 'This is going to be the greatest holiday of my husband's life.'

'I'm afraid she's hard of hearing,' explained Bodie, 'and she thinks eveybody else is as well. Her voice is enough to wake the dead.'

He looked at Mrs Roper. 'Would you mind looking after Mrs Arkwright, Mrs Roper?' he said, recognising her as the wife of his bookmaker, Sydney Roper.

'Of course I will,' she said. 'How wonderfully romantic that she wants to take her husband on holiday with her even though he's dead. There are some husbands who don't want to take their wives on holiday with them even when they're alive.'

She gave Sydney a withering look.

'Listen, my man,' said Mrs Blunt to Farquhar, 'how long is it before this plane of yours takes off? You have got us here at an unholy hour and there is not a sign of the flight being called. This is all stealing time out of our holiday, and you can rest assured that my husband will be demanding a refund. Isn't that right, Stanley?'

'Quite right, dear,' Stanley meant to say, while he actually said, 'Shut up, you old cow.'

'What was that, Stanley?' Mrs Blunt said, unable to believe her ears.

'I said they've shut up now,' he said, his mind in overdrive.

'Shut up what now?'

'The check-in desk,' he said. 'They are not taking any more baggage, so we should be off very soon.'

The airport announcer came to his rescue: 'Attention. Flight Number one two six, Wundatours Airlines. The three o'clock departure for Elsbels will now depart at four fifteen. Departure gate two.'

Farquhar looked at his list. There was one client missing. He was just about to strike his name off when he heard a sound coming from under the check-in desk. 'Psst, here,' the voice said. 'Courier, come here.'

A puzzled Farquhar looked down over the counter, and found himself staring into a thin, bespectacled face poking out from a large kitbag.

'What on earth are you doing there?' he said, departing from his script.

'I'm Bedsop,' he said, 'James Bedsop. Private Investigator.'

Farquhar looked at his clipboard. 'You're my missing client,' he said, now reverting to his robotic role. 'Welcome to Wundatours where everything is wonderful and *you* are the most wonderful of all. I'm Stuart Farquhar, your courier. And you are...'

'I've already told you,' said Bedsop, looking furtively around. 'Now listen, I am on a top-secret assignment and I do not want any of the other members of your party to know I'm here.'

'This is most unorthodox,' said Farquhar. 'I can't possibly hide you away on the plane.'

'I've cleared it with your head office,' said Bedsop, much to the courier's anger and frustration. 'You don't have to hide me away. I am a master of disguise. Nobody will know that it is me on the plane with you. I will appear in a variety of roles during the week. Please do not shout out to me in case it blows my cover.'

Farquhar shrugged. The client was always, always right regardless. 'Anything you say, Mr Bedsop,' he said. 'Can you please now make your way through passport control and into the departure lounge. I'm going to the bar to have a good stiff drink.'

Since joining Wundatours he had become terrified of flying. He needed a drink to steady his nerves, and all the holidaymakers would have joined him had they shared his knowledge of what was in store.

Surely, he thought to himself, he could have made more use of that domestic science degree.

It was six fifteen before the tired and irritable Wundatours holidaymakers were at last summoned to board their flight. Only Mr Arkwright boarded on schedule.

They came out of the terminal building into a gale-force wind and were almost blown across the tarmac towards a smart BAC Super 1-11 airliner. Farquhar, having found time because of the flight delay for half a dozen stiff drinks, raced ahead of them and pointed them past the BAC 1-11 to another aircraft fifty yards beyond it. Ivor Bodie gaped in disbelief. 'Betty!' he shouted. 'That's Betty Grable.'

The other members of the group did not know what he was talking about as they battled against the wind to the propellered plane which was painted in the salmon-pink colours of the Wundatours travel company. If they could have scratched beneath the top layer of paint they would have found the green and brown camouflage colours of a war plane.

'This is Betty Grable,' Bodie was explaining to Biddle as they climbed the rickety steps that took them into the belly of the plane. 'It was the Dakota troop transporter that took me and three hundred other parachutists into France in 1944. I don't care what colour they paint it, I would recognise the old crate anywhere. She took all the flak the Krauts could aim at her and still came through for us. What a lovely old ship.'

It was the most enthusiastic Biddle had known him outside the embalming room where he talked with the same passion about the corpses he was preparing for the ground. He could not help feeling that the plane he was just entering was in need of the last rites and a lot of embalming work. Betty Grable needed new legs.

Old cinema seats had been substituted for the forms on which the troops used to sit, and the inside of the plane was decorated in the same salmon-pink as the outside. A Spanish air stewardess, dressed all in pink so that you could hardly see her against the pink background, welcomed each of them aboard, her wide smile revealing that at least three of her front teeth were missing.

'Which is non-smoking?' asked Mrs Blunt.

'*Qué?*' said the air hostess, who would not see fifty again.

'The non-smoking,' said Mrs Blunt.

'Nicht der fumer, s'il vous plaît, señorita,' said Stanley Blunt, trying out his range of languages.

'Ah,' said the hostess. 'All over smoke.'

The Blunts gave up, and sat in the middle on the port

side. Or behind the driver, as Mrs Blunt put it.

The holidaymakers had just settled into their seats when they were astonished to be joined by an Elvis Presley look alike. 'Hi, folks,' he said with a wave of his heavily ringed fingers before sitting himself down right at the front. For somebody who did not want to be noticed, James Bedsop appeared to be taking a very high profile.

Next on board came a man wearing a pilot's uniform. It was not the uniform or his huge white handlebar moustache that took the eye of the passengers quite so much as his dark glasses and white stick. He tapped his way down the aisle, stumbling over Bernie Biddle's large feet before reaching the door to the cockpit. Behind him, the holidaymakers were speechless with a mixture of shock and fear.

The pilot turned and faced down the aisle, and started to laugh manically. He whipped off his glasses and threw down his stick. 'Just my little joke, folks,' he said. 'We'll soon have this old bus up in the air and we should be divebombing Elsbels at about nine hundred hours.'

'Stinker Winterbottom!' said Bodie, with sudden recognition. 'I thought you'd bought it years ago.'

The pilot peered down the aisle, proving that his eyesight was not one hundred per cent. He finally recognised Bodie. 'Well I'll kiss Hermann Goering's bottom,' he said. 'If it's not Mr Death himself, Ivor Bodie. Haven't clapped eyes on you since we dropped you at Normandy. Still burying 'em, old bean?'

Bodie nodded. 'And are you still bombing 'em?' he asked. 'I think you gave undertakers more work during the war than any other bomber pilot.'

'I'll see you for a drink at the other end... if we make it,' said ex-group captain Winterbottom, with a laugh that chilled rather than amused the passengers.

Stuart Farquhar slid shut the Dakota doors, and came down the aisle handing out disembarkation cards.

'I thought this was the age of bleedin' jet travel,' said Sydney Roper. 'You'll need a lot of knicker elastic to get this thing off the ground. Bloody hell, it's prehistoric.'

'It's hardly the Concorde,' added the Very Reverend Bigger, looking to the heavens. 'I doubt very much if even He will fly with us in this contraption.'

Farquhar remembered the company motto: TURN THE NEGATIVE INTO THE POSITIVE AND MAKE BAD NEWS INTO GOOD NEWS.

'Thish ish the mosht reliable aircraft flying the skiesh,' he said, the stiff drinks he had downed making his tongue go to sleep. 'It hash made more flightsh than any other holiday plane you could menshion, and it hashn't crashed oncesh.'

'Och, but there's always got tae be a ferst time,' said Bertie MacConway, 'and if this is the day it's going tae crash I'll wrap your testicles round your neck and make them intae a bow tie.'

'And my husband will sue your company for every penny it's got,' said Mrs Blunt. 'Won't you, dear.'

'They'll never fly another plane,' Stanley meant to say, while he actually said, 'If I get my way, you old bag, I'll push you right out without a parachute.'

'What was that, Stanley?' Mrs Blunt said, sure that

she had not heard him properly.

'I said they should give us an overnight bag and a parachute,' Stanley ad-libbed, sensing that the time was fast approaching when he would pull the doormat from under her.

They all jumped as the engines thundered into life, and the huge dinosaur of a plane started to shake and rattle as the propellors picked up speed.

'We're on our way, Percy,' shouted widow Arkwright. 'Just look at those people. They look just like ants.'

Nobody was in the mood to tell her that they were ants, and that they had not yet taken off. They were also disinterested in the fact that the ants were *inside* an aircraft that had not been properly cleaned and fumigated since the last tourist season.

Moments after the engines started up the cockpit door opened and the captain came out carrying a megaphone. 'Sorry,' he boomed down the aisle, 'but the intercom system is buggered. While the old kite is warming up, I'd just like to welcome you all aboard on behalf of the Luftwaffe... sorry, my little joke... on behalf of Wundatours, the travel company that guarantees you a wonderful time.'

He removed the megaphone from his lips while adding the aside, 'And if you believe that you'll believe anything.'

The captain then continued his megaphone message. 'I'm Captain Horace Winterbottom, and on behalf of my crew – that's my co-pilot Stevie Wonder and airhostess Juanita "I wanna eater" Sanchez – I'd like to wish you an enjoyable flight. We will be flying at a height of, hopefully, more than one thousand feet, and at speeds of up to two hundred miles an hour or even greater if this damned gale-force wind is behind us. But I must warn you that it just might make it a little bumpy, something like when the Jerry flak is flying all around. But what's a little buffeting? At least you'll be able to say you had a buffet on board.'

He laughed, but sensed that there was something of a loss of confidence among his passengers, and decided to cheer them up. 'Do you know why blind men don't parachute? Because it frightens the shyte out of their guide dogs. Why do women parachutists always wear trousers? Because they don't want to whistle on the way down.'

There was nervous laughter among some of the passengers, but Farqhuar considered, rightly, that the majority were not exactly enraptured by the captain's self-described in-flight entertainment. He signalled for him to wind it up.

'Right,' said Captain Winterbottom, 'that's enough from me. I shall now attempt to get this crate off the floor and, hopefully, back down again somewhere near Elsbels. I notice that a few of you appear to be just a mite anxious. Have no worries. This plane has never crashed before, apart from the occasional crash landing. But that was only in wartime when the Jerries were making things a little difficult for us. The Spanish, you will find, are just a little more friendly, provided you are ready to part with all your pesetas.'

Farquhar was now dancing up and down at the rear of the plane giving a studio floor manager's 'cut' signs for all he was worth. He kept miming with his right forefinger across his throat, but the captain continued to drone on and Farquhar sensed that he was bringing some of his passengers near to the point of panic, not least of all himself. He had told head office that it was time they grounded Captain Winterbottom, but the fact that he flew as a hobby and without pay counted heavily in his favour. He just did not want to be parted from his beloved Betty Grable.

The engines were now nicely warmed up, and Winterbottom decided on one more attempt to warm up his audience. 'I'll just end by telling you the one about the pilot who came home from a long-haul assignment to find his wife in bed with the milkman. He knocked the milkman cold, and when he came round he was in the pilot's workshop. He had screwed the milkman's John Thomas into a vice as tight as he could and had then thrown the handle away. He was standing sharpening a big carving knife. "God," blurted the milkman, "You're not going to cut it off are you?" The pilot handed him the knife. "No pal," he said, You can do that. I'm going to set fire to the workshop."'

That was the breaking point for Farquhar, who had taken another quick swig from the on-board drinks consignment to try to get him through the coming ordeal. He hustled down the aisle and snatched the megaphone from the pilot. 'Thank you, Captain, for that unique in-flight cabaret,' he said. 'I can asshure all of you that you would not get that with any other airline. While the Captain preparesh for take-off I will hand over to Juanita, who will go through the compulshory shafety rulesh.'

He handed the megaphone to Juanita. 'Liedeez and genitalsmen,' she began, which were about the only words that anybody understood as she gave the routine saftey demonstration. When she showed how to put on the lifejacket, Sadie Tompkins said, 'You wouldn't see me dead wearing that. I never wear yellow.'

Juanita mimed blowing the whistle attached to the lapel of the lifejacket. 'Blows thees withel when you ares in the acqua mineral,' she said.

'What a joke,' said Sydney Roper. 'You're down in the sea about to drown and they expect you to start playing the bloody penny whistle. What tune should we play, "For those in peril on the sea?"'

'Shut up while...' started Gladys Golightly One.

'We're listening to the emergency guidelines,' finished Gladys Golightly Two.

'You will stick your oar in,' Ethel Roper hissed.

'They don't give you an oar, just a flipping whistle,' he grumbled. 'Your last act would be blowing up as if for off-side.'

'You could always attract help with your wolf whistle, Mr Roper,' Sadie said with a cackling laugh.

It will, silently vowed Ethel, soon be the last whistle for her.

To say that the 1939-built Dakota took off smoothly would be as accurate as saying that the *Titanic* made a graceful exit. It *shuddered* off, and the shaking was such that Ivor Bodie's false teeth jumped out and bit Bernie Biddle on the thigh. The plane hit more pockets than you would find in a snooker hall, and every time it dipped into an air pocket the Golightly sisters screamed, first of all Gladys One quickly followed by Gladys Two. Elvis Presley sang 'All Shook Up'.

Juanita did her best to serve the in-flight meal of plastic beef with plastic roast potatoes and plastic carrots. She managed only to hurl it around the interior as if in an Olympic throwing event every time the plane lurched. All the passengers finished wearing the food, which fortunately did not stain because of its frozen condition. Those who did manage to get any mouthfuls down were quickly bringing them up, and Captain Winterbottom and Percy Arkwright were the only passengers who did not need the sickbag during a flight that, to use Sydney Roper's rather colourful description, 'had more ups and downs than a Soho tart's drawers.'

The arrival at Elsbels was, to say the least, spectacular. Captain Winterbottom did not so much come in to land as to attack the airport. Spanish ground crew threw themselves to the ground as he made two wild passing movements before thumping the plane down at the third attempt. The captain was laughing like a mad man at the controls. 'That frightened the shyte out of them,' he said. 'That will teach them not to put me into a stacking queue in future.'

His passengers behind did not hear his comments. They were all kneeling and too engrossed in their prayers led by the Very Reverend Francis Bigger. Elvis led them in a chorus of 'Abide With Me'.

Ashen-faced Farquhar, shaken back to sobriety, remembered company policy: TURN THE NEGATIVE INTO THE POSITIVE AND MAKE BAD NEWS INTO GOOD NEWS.

'The beauty of that flight,' he said, 'was that it will make all future flights seem extremely tolerable and the holiday can now only get better.'

Everybody was too relieved to have landed in one piece – and were still trying to find their stomachs let alone their voices – to make any comment.

Francis Bigger summed up the majority of feelings when he made a sign with his fingers in the direction of the cockpit. And it was not the sign of the cross.

There was one slight hold up as the travel-weary Wundatours party came through passport control and then customs. The officials insisted that they wanted the coffin opened.

'But he's got no sun cream on,' shouted widow Arkwright. 'And this is his time of day when he has a nap.'

Despite the protests the lid was prised open. Ivor Bodie had packed Percy Arkwright in so quickly that he did not realise that the shroud had become caught in the lid, and as it was pulled open the figure of Mr Arkwright rose with it. There were screams and shouts from the passengers waiting to come through customs, and one woman customs officer fainted at the sight of the old boy sitting up in the coffin with what appeared to be a crooked grin on his face.

'Oh, Percy,' shouted Mrs Arkwright, 'you do look well. I knew this holiday would do you good.'

The coffin was eventually cleared after Percy's passport had been produced to prove he was who they claimed he was. In fact, it was the only time he had ever looked like his passport photo.

Bodie and Biddle, with Sydney Roper and Bertie MacConway helping as pall bearers, carried the coffin to the waiting coach that was going to take the holidaymakers to their hotel, which was in the same road as the Chapel of Rest.

The coach was even older than the Dakota plane, and the baggage hold was not big enough to take the coffin. It was finally roped to the top of the coach by a driver called Pedro, who had been taught just four words of English. 'Steek your facking teeps,' he kept saying, holding out a hand and looking suprised when nothing was put into it.

'How far away is our hotel?' asked Sadie Tompkins.

'Oh, only about a one hour drive,' said Farquhar, knowingly out in his assessment by an hour or so.

'But it said in the brochure "just a short ride" from the airport,' moaned Mrs Blunt.

'Well it is not far in actual distance,' said Farquhar, 'but the mountain road is only single lane and it can sometimes be tiresome if we get stuck behind a mule and cart.'

'This is not good enough,' said Mrs Blunt. 'We have the very latest Austin Allegro at home, and now we're having to travel in a vehicle that looks as if it was used in the Spanish Civil War.'

'I congratulate you on your observation, Mrs Blunt,' said Farquhar, once again turning the negative into the positive. 'This was used by General Franco to transport his personal staff around Elsbels, and we have booked it to give you all a feel of Spanish history.'

The fact that it cost a quarter of the price of a modern

coach to hire did not, of course, come into the equation at all.

The coach did very well indeed considering its age and condition. It actually almost got to the top of the mountain climb through narrow winding roads with terrifying drops on either side before it coughed and spat its last and refused to go another yard.

And so it was that what looked like a funeral cortège, led by a man in a sickly salmon-pink blazer, came slowly down the moutain road in single file. Sydney Roper and Stanley Blunt kindly gave a hand in helping to carry the coffin. Elvis walked ahead of the coffin singing 'Crying in the Chapel'. 'Heartbreak Hotel' would come later.

'Just think how much worse it could have been,' said Farquhar at his most positive. 'We could have been climbing up the mountain road. At least the descent is easier on the legs and lungs, and just look at that beautiful view.'

'I'm famished,' said Sydney Roper.

'Yes,' said Bernie Biddle. 'I could eat an 'orse.'

Farquhar kept to himself the fact that he just might have that delicacy offered to him before their seven-day sentence was finished.

Their destination, which they would reach only seven hours behind schedule, was the Hotel Grande Elsbels situated half a mile from the bottom of the mountain road.

This was where their holiday, and their troubles, would *really* start.

Elsbels, Thursday

Dear Mildred,
Me and your Dad arrived safe and well. The plane was bumpy, but your Dad didn't complain once. The hotel seems very nice, and it will be better when we get lights, water and food. There are too many foreign people here for my taste, but it's doing your Dad the world of good. I am looking forward to picking up a few things at the shops. Don't forget to put the cat out. Love

Mum XXXXX

Miss Mildred Arkwright,

27a Desmond Tutu House,

Hackneyway Heath,

London E26,

England, Great Britain .

2

ELSBELS, WEDNESDAY 30 MAY 1973

IT was nearly six o'clock in the evening when Stuart Farquhar finally led his dispirited party through the gates and up the drive to the entrance to the Hotel Grande Elsbels, which nestled three quarters of the way down the highest mountain in the Costa del Sol region most recently turned into a tourist trap. The holidaymakers should have been there for late breakfast, and had made it in time for an early dinner. Waiting at the bottom of the steps to greet them were Pepe and Floella Ripoffola, the husband and wife who managed the hotel for the syndicate that owned the Grande Elsbels. They had one extra in their group in the boxed shape of Percy Arkwright. The Chapel of Rest had been closed, and so they had no alternative but to bring the coffin with them.

Pepe bowed and Floella curtsied as the weary, dust-choked tourists trudged into view, dragging their cases with them. Only widow Arkwright, and, of course, Percy, were spared the walk from the coach, which was exhausting even though the two-mile journey was mostly downhill (or, rather, down mountainside). Mrs Arkwright had arrived straddled across her husband's coffin, the front of which was borne on the wide shoulders of Bernie Biddle, with the other men in the party taking turns shouldering the back end in shifts of two at a time.

'Señor Farque,' said Pepe in warm greeting, pumping

Farquhar's hand as if he was expecting to produce water. 'Eet ees so long seence I sees you. Welcomes, welcomes, welcomes to new Hotel Grande Elsbels.'

He looked at the new arrivals gathered behind Farquhar like a huddled mass that would not have looked out of place on Ellis Island. 'And my wifes Floella and me, Pepe, we welcomes all you peoples as first guests of our new and much splendeed hotel,' he said, grinning broadly with a sunshine smile that revealed a flashing gold middle tooth and which radiated warmth to the holidaymakers. Warmth they did not need. They were already boiling hot after their trek in the late afternoon sun that scorched them all the way down the mountain road.

Their arrival had been greeted by a temperature a mere fifty-four degrees above the 20 degrees Fahrenheit that they had left behind at Luton. Mr and Mrs Blunt, in their heavy tweed coats, were particularly affected by the heat.

Tears welled in Pepe's eyes as he looked at the coffin with a combination of curiosity and sympathy. 'Somebody's dies?' he said. 'Must be food on airplanes again, yes?'

'No, no, no,' said Farquhar, appalled at the suggestion. 'This is Mr Arkwright, and he has a double room booked with his wife.'

Pepe looked horrified. 'He sleeps in our new beds?' he said. 'But, Señor Farque, thees wood, eet would tears our shits.'

'It is only for one night,' said Farquhar. 'He will be transferred to the Chapel of Rest tomorrow. Meantime you can put him up in a spare room. There is no need for a bed.'

'Tennees table room,' said Mrs Rippoffola, whose very clipped, abbreviated English was better than her husband's apart from the fact that she transposed the main words of each sentence and, like Pepe, she had never been taught the definite article. 'Man dead can table on rest.'

Bodie and Biddle carried the coffin to the table tennis room. They arranged it across the middle of the table in place of the net, so that residents could still play if they wished. So far it had not been much of a holiday for Mr Arkwright.

'I canna wait to get into a cold shower, change into a fresh kilt and then enjoy a leisurely meal and a pint or three of the local brew,' said Bertie MacConway.

'You and me both, Jock,' said Sydney Roper. 'A nice cold shower followed by an even nicer ice-cold glass of sangria.'

Pepe looked more mournful than professional mourner Ivor Bodie. 'Señors,' he said, wringing his hands, 'sadly I haves to tell you that waters, eet ees not colds.'

'All right, a warm shower will do,' said Sydney.

More wringing of the hands. 'Eet ees not warms either,' said Pepe. 'All waters off.'

'Well switch it back on,' said Farquhar rather tersely. 'These honoured guests of ours need a shower before they sit down to dinner.'

Now both Pepe and Floella were wringing their hands in unison. 'Very sorrys, Señor Farque,' Pepe said, his face a picture of misery. 'No waters and no dinners.'

'What, no dinners?' said Farquhar, unable to believe what he was hearing.

'This is a disgrace,' said Mrs Blunt.

'A disgrace,' said Mr Blunt, both his mind and tongue in agreement with his wife for the first time in months.

The rest of the Wundatours party had energy left only to murmur their agreement, apart from Bertie MacConway. 'Somebody is going tae get a Glasgie kiss before this nicht is through,' he said. 'Big Mac is getting mad.'

The Golightly sisters were impressed. They each wondered, Gladys One a split second ahead of Gladys Two, what a Glasgie kiss was and which one of them would be the first to get it.

The Very Reverend Bigger made the sign of the cross at Pepe, using a fist rather than a finger and he had to be restrained by the Blunts. Now there's a novelty.

'We are sorry terribly,' said Floella. 'Waters, electrics and gasses have been off switched.'

'Why?' said Farquhar.

'We have paid not pesetas,' said Floella.

'We waits for you to arrives, Señor Farque, to brings us money,' said Pepe. 'We expects you thees mornings, but you are no heres and off goes our waters, electrics and gasses. Now eet weell be mañana befores we are switches back on.'

Mañana. This was to become the first Spanish word that the tourists would regularly recognise.

'What are you going to do...' started Gladys Golightly One.

'...about feeding us,' finished Gladys Two.

Pepe looked as if he was seeing and hearing double, which he was. 'My wifes weel prepares for you bests beesceets in Elsbels,' he said, flashing the golden smile.

'And what about the sangria?' said Sydney Roper. 'I want a jugful brought to my room. Not mañana, but *this* yana.'

The wringing hands. 'Sorry Señor, but no sangria and no rooms,' said Pepe, hanging his head like a naughty dog knowing he was going to get a scolding from his master. He was not disappointed.

'No rooms?' said Farquhar, his voice going up two octaves. 'What the hell d'you mean, no rooms? You, sir, are a disgrace to your hotel profession and I will be making a full report of this to the Wundatours complaints committee.'

This committee actually consisted of one person sitting in front of a wastepaper basket filing the complaints. It was a full-time job.

'Rooms ready not,' explained Floella. 'Workersmen left afternoon thees and I not time have to rooms do.'

Farquhar, like all well-trained couriers, had been taught to think on his feet. TURN ALL NEGATIVES INTO POSITIVES, AND MAKE GOOD NEWS OUT OF BAD NEWS.

'Good,' he said brightly. 'There's a wonderful little Spanish restaurant just a brief walk away that will give you the authentic feel and taste of Spain. While the lovely Floella here is preparing our rooms, I will take you there for a splendid meal and several jugs of sangria on Wundatours. Leave the cases here, and the hotel porters can stack them in the baggage room until we return.'

There was, in these early days of package holidays nothing quite so resilient as a British holidaymaker abroad. Give him, more so than her, the promise of a meal and a free drink and he would find that extra spurt of energy necessary to cross any barrier. The women were not quite so easily bought.

'My feet are killing me,' said Sadie Tompkins from high up on her platform shoes on which she had somehow negotiated the downhill walk. 'I couldn't walk another inch.'

Bernie Biddle won the rush to offer to carry her, and it was a considerably cheered up party that started out on the 'brief' walk to the restaurant. A hotel trolley was provided to wheel Mrs Arkwright along, and the Golightly sisters attached themselves to an arm each of Bertie MacConway, who was silently tossing up in his mind as to which sister to spend the first night with.

'I wonder what you have...' started Gladys One.

'Under that kilt of yours,' finished Gladys Two.

'That's for you tae find out in the fullness of time,' said MacConway, 'but let's just say that they dinna call me Big Mac for nothing.'

The walk was quite a lot farther than Farquhar – or Farque, as they were now all calling him – remembered from his last visit to Elsbels eight months before at the end of the previous season. Since then they had not only built the Hotel Grande Elsbels but had started on several more and all the old familiar landmarks had gone, along with the character of what had been a quaint corner of old Spain. The new vista of half-built and soon to be started multi-storey hotels had distorted his perception of distance. He could not really argue with Stanley Blunt's shrewd assessment that it resembled a building site.

It was forty-eight minutes later when they at last reached the quaint-looking restaurant, the walk being made less laborious by choruses of 'Blue Suede Shoes' from Elvis. The mood of the party, it had to be said, was not helped when it was discovered that the restaurant would not be opened for business until the following Monday. A notice on the door from the proprietors read: GONE TO ENGLAND ON HOLIDAY. BACK JUNE 5.

But just half a mile away the Union Jack Pub, run by Jack and Jill Smith – a couple from Luton – was open for business and never had bangers and mash tasted better. Admittedly the beer was warm, but it was wet and they all had a good laugh as they discussed the day's adventures. The good old Brits. This was the spirit of the Blitz shining through. They could get to quite like this Spanish lifestyle.

Everybody seemed to have an enjoyable time, with the exception of Mrs Blunt who did not stop moaning. 'I would not be seen dead in a place like this back home in Guildford,' she said. 'We only ever drink in the Conservative club, isn't that right Stanley?'

'Yes, dear,' he meant to say, but it came out as, 'I hope your drink will choke you.'

'What was that?' she said, her tongue suddenly an icicle.

'I just said this is all a joke,' he ad-libbed, sinking another pint of best bitter in the hope that it would control his urge to throttle her. Or, even more hopefully, that it would give him the Dutch courage to go through with the deed.

The only slightly souring note during the evening was when Ethel Roper slapped Sadie Tompkins around the face after she had caught her having a quick grope in the pool room with Sydney. But they were quickly pulled apart, the ladies that is, and Elvis soon brought the party back to life with a medley of his greatest hits.

The Very Reverend Bigger, shifting beer by the gallon, led them all in a jolly hokey cokey, and Gladys and Gladys Golightly sang, fairly predictably, 'Sisters' but with the slight twist that they performed it to the tune of 'The Stripper' and were only persuaded to keep their bras and panties on by the fact that a cold evening wind was sending an icy breeze through the bar.

Only widow Arkwright and Ivor Bodie did not join in the dancing. The nearest Bodie came to getting into the party rhythm was that his teeth were clattering like Spanish castanets as he talked, and occasionally they would jump out into his beer. The rumour was that rather than pay out for a set of his own he had removed the teeth from a client who would have had no further use for them.

Bodie, who could have bored for Britain, was propped at the corner of the bar not noticing that his audience had left him for the dance floor. He was chuntering on about how in years to come this area of Spain would be owned by the Krauts, and that the Brits would be confined to ghetto areas where gun-toting luger louts would turn holidays into nightmares. Bodie fancied himself as something of a prophet, and only time would tell that he was at least ten per cent accurate with his forecasts.

Out on the dance floor Gladys and Gladys Golightly were getting MacConway to twirl faster and faster in a bid to find out what was under that kilt. If it was a Big Mac, they had yet to catch a glimpse of it. Bertie was determined to give one of the sisters a full display before the night was through. But which one? Would it be the psychopath?

After sinking more drinks than she was used to, Ethel Roper was the prime mover in an energetic performance of 'Knees Up Mother Brown', and she did her best to bring her knees up into Sydney's groin while they were leaping around the dance floor.

So their first night in Spain had developed into a good old British knees-up and made everybody feel at home, except Mrs Blunt. 'We don't go in for this sort of thing in Guildford,' she said. 'My husband and I only dance old-time, don't we Stanley?'

Stanley did not answer. He was too busy doing the twist with a very merry Sadie Tompkins, and he was in danger of having his eyes knocked out by her leading points as she jigged around in Farque's salmon-pink blazer. This was the sort of danger Stanley Blunt wanted more of, and he was now wondering whether it would be accepted if his wife were to stumble on the way back to the hotel and fall down the mountainside. But he had heard too many horrific stories of what went on in Spanish jails, and decided that the risk was not worth it. But his moment would come. It was just a question of time.

It was only when they returned to the Hotel Grande Elsbels four hours later, in a drink-induced happy mood, that somebody remembered they had left Mrs Arkwright on the baggage trolley in the saloon bar of the Union Jack. The old dear was fast asleep by the time Bernie Biddle returned to collect her.

She woke up with a kick start when he began pushing her up the mountain, and had obviously come out of a graphic dream.

'What the facking hell are you doing, Percy Arkwright?' she shouted, making Biddle jump with shock. 'I told you not here in the air raid shelter.'

Back at the Grande Elsbels they were collecting their cases from where they had left them at the bottom of the steps, and were making their way to their rooms up staircases and along corridors that were lit by candles.

Ask any travel courier, and he or she will tell you that the time they dread most is the two hours after booking a party into their hotel. They call it the 'Moan Zone'. And for Stuart Farquhar the moans came thick and fast.

The Blunts, naturally, were first to complain. 'We want sheets on our bed,' she told Pepe, quite reasonably.

He was outraged. 'No, señora,' he said, 'you must do eet in toileet not on beds.'

She and Stanley stumbled down the darkened stairs to moan to Farquhar, who had taken up a position at the reception desk so that he could field what he guessed were going to be many complaints. 'There are no sheets on our bed,' grumbled Mrs Blunt.

'But all the beds have duvets,' said Farquhar.

'We don't want any of that foreign rubbish,' said Mrs Blunt. 'We want good old British blankets and sheets like we have at home in Guildford, best quality linen, of course.'

'Just for tonight, Mrs Blunt,' pleaded Farquhar, I would greatly appreciate it if you would make do with the duvets. I will see to it that you get your blankets and sheets from tomorrow night.'

'This is not good enough,' said Mrs Blunt. 'First there were the delays at that dreary Luton Airport, then an aeroplane in which you would not fly pigs...'

'But it flew you,' thought both Farquhar and Stanley.

'...then a coach from the airport that was like a deathtrap on the mountainside, and then a walk down a mountain when we could have suffered sunstroke...'

'Yes, but...' said Farquhar, trying to turn the negative into the positive.

'...and now an hotel without food, electricity or running water, or sheets and blankets.'

It was, Farquhar had to admit to himself, a pretty fair summary of the holiday so far.

'Yes,' he managed to interject, 'but what you are getting for your twenty-nine pounds a head price is a feel of the *real* Spain and the slightly haphazard yet beautifully spontaneous way that they live.'

'Thirty-one pounds a head,' corrected Mrs Blunt. 'Don't forget our two pounds extra for a seaview, and there had better be a good view of the sea when we can finally see out of our window tomorrow or I will set my Stanley loose. You're a terror when you're aroused, aren't you Stanley?'

'Yes dear,' Stanley meant to say, but it came out as, 'The last time I was aroused was on our wedding night when I managed to talk you into removing your fleecy-lined bloomers, and quickly wished I hadn't bothered. It was the biggest let down since Josephine said, "Not tonight, Napoleon".'

'What on earth are you waffling on about?' snapped Mrs Blunt, thinking that all the foreign drink she had poured down her throat at that dreadful Union Jack place must have affected her hearing.

'I was just saying what a disappointment it has all been,' said Stanley.

The next complaint came from the Very Reverend Bigger. 'Listen, my son,' he said to Farquhar, 'I can put up with not having electricity or water, but I *do* insist on having walls in my room.'

'Stop mucking about,' said Farquhar with a grin, thinking – no, hoping – that his leg was being pulled.

'This is no joke, my son,' said Bigger. 'I'm telling you that there is only the front wall in my room. 'They are still building the fourth floor of this place. Could have fallen and broken my neck. I shall sue Wundatours for every penny they've got.'

'My humble apologies,' said a shocked Farquhar. 'I shall check this out first thing in the morning when we can all see properly. Meantime, I shall get a mattress put on the floor in the table tennis room so that you can get your head down tonight.'

'I'd rather have my head down with Miss Tompkins,' he said, then smacked his wrist for the filthy thought.

A protesting, pyjamaed Pepe was summoned to bring

a mattress. 'Thees will be hextra,' he said. It was the first time the phrase had been heard.

'Ignore him, it is his idea of a little joke,' said Farquhar, sincerely hoping that he was right in his assessment as Pepe led them to the table tennis room. He opened the door, and then let out a yell, dropped the mattress and scuttled off. In the flickering light of a candle on the table tennis table, they could make out the shadowy figure of Percy Arkwright sitting up in his coffin. Mrs Arkwright was alongside him telling him about the day's adventures.

Farquhar quietly pulled the door to, and the mattress for the Very Reverend Bigger was laid on the dining room floor. He went to sleep after literally drinking in everything in his Bible.

Sydney Roper was next with a moan. He wanted to complain about having his wife in the same room as him, but confined his beef to the fact that there was no glass in their balcony window. Farquhar was just relieved to hear that they had a balcony. 'But you will benefit from that during the day when it is searingly hot,' he said.

'But there's a facking perishing cyclone of wind coming through what should be the window,' said a blue-lipped Roper, who was discovering just how cold Spanish nights could get once the sun had surrendered.

'Ah,' said Farquhar, 'that's a brilliantly conceived cooling system thought of by a Spanish builder called Juan Brickatatime. He is trying to introduce it instead of air conditioning, and perhaps at the end of the holiday you would be so kind as to give your assessment of the method. If you do not feel it has worked to your satisfaction, I will personally see to it that you and your wife get a two pounds refund. Each.'

Ivor Bodie complained that Elvis in the adjoining room was keeping him awake by singing about having a wooden heart, and Elvis grumbled that Bodie was keeping him awake in the adjoining room by talking incessantly to Bernie Biddle about how they could give the undertaking business a boost by allowing funeral directors to cremate people while they were still alive.

It was two o'clock in the morning when Farquhar at last felt he could retire to his first floor room. He opened his door, undressed in the dark and dropped in near exhaustion on to his bed. The stunned courier was quickly brought to attention by the hand of one of the Golightly sisters. But which one?

In the next room, Bertie MacConway was revealing his Big Mac to the other Golightly sister. But which one? Gladys One, or Gladys Two?

One floor up, Sadie Tompkins was having the holiday of a lifetime. She had stumbled in the dark into the arms of Giorgio, the Grande Elsbels headwaiter who preferred laying guests to laying tables. He dutifully waited on her all night, and she vowed to give him a big tip to match the one she was receiving.

'Go lightly with me, Stuart baby,' said Gladys Golightly One – or was it Two? – to Farquhar. 'I want you to give me a better time than my sister is having with that kilted beast.'

'Go lightly with me, Big Mac, baby,' said Gladys Golightly Two – or was it One? – to MacConway. 'I want you to give me a better time than my sister is having with that pink-blazered pansie.'

MacConway and Farquhar did their best, but each of them found it disconcerting to have the sisters calling through the wall to each other with a running commentary. When they later compared notes, both MacConway and Farquhar described their Golightly twin as having psychopathic tendencies.

The Scot felt it was fairly psychopathic when his Miss Golightly waited until he was asleep and then tied his testicles with a piece of string that she then attached to the door. As she left his room, very disappointed with his performance, she slammed the door shut and MacConway woke everybody in the hotel with a louder yell than was ever heard at Bannockburn. Even Percy Arkwright was said to have raised an eyebrow.

Farquhar felt it was fairly psychopathic when his Miss Golightly waited until he was asleep and then tied his testicles with a piece of string that she then attached to his big toes. She, very disappointed by his performance, then returned to the room she was sharing with her sister. When Farquhar got out of bed some hours later he woke the whole of Elsbels with his screams as he stumbled around the floor like a crazed Quasimodo. It sounded as if he was calling his own nickname at the top of his voice, 'Farque'.

The lesson learned was that it did not pay to disappoint the Golightly sisters. But which one was the psychopath?

Up on the fourth floor, Elvis was singing 'Jailhouse Rock'. He was unconcerned about the absence of walls.

Elsbels, Thursday

Dear Charles,
Having an absolutely wonderful time in a spiffing five-star hotel with every convenience imagineable. The place is packed with bank managers and the like. Our chef is a cordon bleu and we are guzzling champagne like there is no tomorrow. Please make sure our neighbours see this card. Father is in top form and talks the language like a native, Lots of love, **Mother**

Charles Blunt Esquire,

The Laurels,

31 Harkness Estate,

Guildford,

Surrey, England,

United Kingdom.

3

ELSBELS, THURSDAY 1 JUNE 1973

NONE of the newly arrived guests at the Hotel Grande Elsbels had ordered an early-morning call, but they each got one in the rather annoying guise of a dozen pneumatic drills starting in unison at eight o'clock. They produced what could have been an orchestrated cacophony of ear-shattering, earth-trembling noise in the grounds of the hotel and on the adjoining building sites. It was enough to wake the dead and, indeed, widow Arkwright was convinced that she saw her husband wince as she closed the lid on him and prepared to go to the dining room for breakfast.

'What the facking hell...' started Gladys Golightly One.

'Was that?' finished Gladys Golightly Two.

It was the nearest the sisters had got to having the earth move for them since their arrival on the Costa del Sol. Their two dates the previous night had hardly made even the bed move.

Stanley Blunt, who had been dreaming of dropping his wife off the top of the mountain, woke up thinking that he had fallen off with her. He did not expect to make such a crashing noise as he tumbled down the mountainside. It took him several seconds to realise that he was listening to rather than making the noise. First of all he thought that it was Evelyn snoring as usual, but she was sitting up alongside him prodding him in the ribs.

'What are you going to do about it, Stanley?' she said. 'Ring down to reception and tell them to stop that racket immediately.'

He reached for the bedside telephone which had been placed on a cabinet just out of reach of the bed. As he stretched he fell out of the bed with a bump. The telephone, of course, was dead. There was still no electricity.

Stanley stepped out on to the balcony, noticing for the first time the fairly irritating matter that there was no door to the balcony and then the equally aggravating fact that there was no sign of the sea. Lots and lots of sand, but no sea. The sand was piled high alongside growlingly hungry cement mixers as dozens of Spanish construction workers busied themselves building the next hotel and finishing off the one in which the Wundatours holidaymakers were being noisily introduced to their first morning in Elsbels.

Evelyn Blunt was now standing alongside her husband. She was looking around with an open mouth and Stanley had the fleeting thought that she could have starred in a re-make of 'Moby Dick'.

'Go down to reception and ask them where the sea is, right now!' she ordered. 'We've paid extra for a sea view.'

As he was on remote control and programmed to do anything he was told, Stanley found himself opening the door and out in the corridor before he realised that he did not have on a stitch of clothing. He had slept nude because he could not find his pyjamas in the pitch blackness of their room. In fact it had taken he and

Evelyn several minutes and a dozen matches before they even found their beds.

The door had closed to behind him, and as he grasped the fact that he was in a rather embarrassing state of undress he turned and knocked for Evelyn to let him back into the room. As she – a vision in winceyette bloomers, pink corset and thick cotton vest – was still out on the balcony trying to fathom whether her first complaint should be about the infernal noise or the absence of the sea, she could not hear him.

Stanley looked frantically around for cover of some sort, and his eyes fell on a red fire extinguisher attached to the wall. He unclipped it and held it in front of him like a warrior's shield as he crept along the corridor looking for something a little more suitable with which to hide his embarrassment.

He was approaching the top of the marble-tiled staircase when he was unfortunate enough to tread on a loose carpet tack. The extinguisher slipped from his hands as he hopped around trying to remove the tack from between his toes, and the release lever hit the brass handrail on the staircase leading down to reception. An unsuspecting Pepe was going about his business by the reception desk, one floor below, when a gallon of white foam suddenly enveloped him as the extinguisher clattered down the stairs.

By the time he had wiped the foam from his eyes and looked up there was no sign of how or why the extinguisher had made its sudden attack. Already, he sensed, the British guests were makings troubles. He had dealt with revolting Brits before in a previous hotel that he and his wife had run before it was closed down as a condemned building, and as he set about cleaning up the ankle-deep foam in reception he braced himself for more trouble. This time he would be ready for them. He had made contingency plans.

Stanley meanwhile had bumped into a heavy-eyed Giorgio, who was making his escape from the demands of the insatiable Sadie Tompkins. Seeing his predicament, Giorgio kindly lent Stanley his waiter's tea towel and then followed him to his room and unlocked the door with his pass key. To Giorgio this was just another loco Englishman. To his mind, all the British men were crazy, and all the women lovely. Well, most of them. He was about to meet one of the unlovely ones.

Evelyn thought Giorgio had been sent to appease her. 'In here you,' she ordered in a booming she-who-must-be-obeyed voice that could make a parade of guards stand to attention.

'*Si*?' said Giorgio.

'Exactly,' said Evelyn. 'Where is it?'

'*Si*?' said a bewildered Giorgio.

'Sea, sea, sea!' roared Evelyn. 'Where is it? We've paid extra to see the sea.'

'*Si*?' repeated Giorgio, who was not quite sure he was up to this ordeal after his pleasant but strenuous night with the señorita down the corridor, whatever her name was.

'Don't stand there repeating sea like a Spanish parrot,' said a near apoplectic Mrs Blunt. 'Just show me where it is.'

She dragged poor Giorgio out on to the balcony. 'So

where is it, eh?' she shouted above the thunder of the drills. 'Where's the sea?'

Evelyn mimed as if swimming, and as she swung her arms around her head Giorgio was convinced he was in the presence of a psychopath (but that treat was yet to come).

It finally dawned on him just what it was that the mad woman wanted.

'Hah,' he beamed. 'Sea, *si*?'

'Sea, sea?' said Evelyn. 'Just the sea will do. Where is it?'

Giorgio bent himself over the balcony, craned his neck and looked to his right and pointed.

'There she ees,' he said triumphantly. 'Eet ees sea, *si*?'

With great difficulty, Evelyn leant her formidable frame over the balcony, craned her neck in a similar way to how Giorgio had done and, yes, there it was a mile or so to the right. The sea. It could just be made out at the foot of the mountain road.

This, of course, was not good enough for a professional complainer like Mrs Blunt. 'We have paid extra to see the sea without having to risk our life and limb leaning over a balcony above a building site,' she said, as she shoved Giorgio back into the room with the palm of her hand. 'What are you going to do about it?

'*Si*?' said the unfortunate Giorgio.

'Enough about the sea,' said Evelyn. 'I just want to know what you are going to do about refunding the extra money we paid.'

'Hah, hextra,' said Giorgio, at last understanding one of the words being machine gunned at him. His English was, he had to admit, poor but he always understood what the ladies wanted. 'You no wants me. You wants to talks manager. He hin charge of hextras. I honly waiters. Tea, coffee, sank you ma'am.'

Giorgio gave a half bow, and looked more the part of the waiter when the now-dressed Stanley placed the tea towel back over his arm. He also gave him ten pesetas, which on the rate of exchange at the time was all of threepence. Giorgio bowed again on a backwards retreat from the room and from the mad woman and the loco man who liked to hop around the corridors without any clothes. The crazy Eengleesh.

'Why on earth are you tipping him?' said Evelyn. 'Like so many foreigners, he can't even speak English properly.'

Ask any travel courier, and he or she will tell you that the second worst time that they dread is the first two or three hours of the morning when their never-satisfied clients are preparing to start the first full day of their holiday. They call this The First Morning Moan Zone.

The complaints came tumbling in for Farquhar, who was still recovering from his disturbing encounter with the Golightly sister, Gladys One or Two. He was still not sure which one but whichever one it was he would make sure he avoided her for the remainder of the holiday. He had broken one of his own self-imposed rules that no client should be slept with before the final night, but he had no option as the twin, whichever one it was, had smuggled herself into his bed without an invitation. Now he was sitting here having to listen to complaints, when he himself had cause for the biggest complaint of all. He had been assaulted, but dare not say a word to a soul because it was a company rule that couriers should not sleep with clients, not even on the final night. Not that he had slept much of the night with Miss Golightly. She had kept him awake with her demands, and also her shouted conversations through the wall with her sister.

The top ten main moans from the clients noted down on a memorandum pad by Farquhar were:

1) About the noise;
2) About the breakfast (dried biscuits and lemonade);
3) Having to step over the still sleeping Very Reverend Bigger on his mattress in the dining room;
4) Still no water and electricity;
5) Workmen hammering on the fourth and fifth floors;
6) The marble reception floor being dangerously slippery with foam;
7) The lack of glass in windows and missing doors to balconies;
8) Wardrobes with no backs to them, so that when you opened them you were looking into the adjoining room;
9) Toilets that, naturally with the water switched off, would not flush;
10) And, of course, the lack of views of the sea and the chorused complaints of, 'Where's the beach?'

Farquhar silenced the Blunts on their moans about the sea view by guaranteeing a refund of half their supplement, which they reluctantly agreed was fair after the demonstration from Giorgio that the sea was just about visible.

The mass moan about the missing beach was just a little bit harder to get round because they were all producing the Wundatours holiday brochure that clearly showed a photograph of the Grande Elsbels with the sea lapping at the beach just a few yards from the front of the hotel. Farquhar had to resort to pointing out the smallprint in the brochure which stated:

> All photographs in this brochure are artists' impressions that give only an approximate guide to the hotel and the proximity of the sea and beach. Wundatours will not be held liable for any damages or compensation for any facts that may prove even slightly misleading, and will take immediate and positive legal action against any client who spreads any malicious gossip about Wundatours and/or its employees and associates. You have been warned. Enjoy a wonderful holiday with Wundatours.

This did not stop them moaning, but there was a definite lessening of the malicious edge in their comments. Stanley Blunt, who had studied law for six months before deciding to switch to a career as an accounts clerk after getting *nil point* in his first exam, now took the precaution of prefacing everything he said to Farquhar or the Grande Elsbels employees, 'I reserve all rights...' This seemed just a little absurd when he was, for instance, asking for something as simple as a beach towel ('I reserve all rights, but can I please have a beach towel'). But with his expertish knowledge of the law he was determined to protect himself against any legal threat now that he knew that Wundatours was obviously a litigious type of company.

There was another fairly mooted moan about the lack of staff. Pepe answered this for the beleaguered Farquhar. 'Eet ees not full season, yet,' he explained. 'When parents comes with childreens in school holidays then I doubles staffs, but thees is low season and we have staffs enoughs for everytheengs.'

His wife, Floella, might have disagreed with this assessment had she the time to join in any conversation. She was in charge of the cooking and the cleaning, and was deputy to Pepe on the reception desk. Giorgio had the grand title of head waiter, but was in fact the only waiter. He was also the porter and the barman, as well as the unofficial gigolo.

One major complaint was sorted out by Farquhar with money from his own pocket following Pepe's insistence that the lemonade served at breakfast was 'a hextra'. It was the breaking point for Bertie MacConway, already in a foul mood after his traumatic experience with the Golightly sister. When Pepe said he would have to pay 'hextra' for the lemonade, he pinned the hotel manager up against a wall and was about to deliver the 'Glasgie kiss' when Farquhar intervened. He paid Pepe for a dozen full bottles of lemonade, and also gave him the money to settle the outstanding electricity and water bills to ensure that all services would be restored that afternoon.

The next moan was fairly predictable. The Golightly sisters were the first to be disappointed when going for an early morning dip (not to be confused with what went on the previous night). They came marching together into reception in eye-catching bikinis that had caused a dropping off of the workrate of the construction workers drilling alongside the pool.

'There is no...' started Gladys Golightly One.

'Water in the pool,' finished Gladys Golightly Two, who had bruises on her bottom from where she had lowered herself into the pool. She was just relieved that she had not entered with her usual swallow dive.

'Hah,' said Pepe, 'many apologees but water has not yet been deliver-red. Water shortage on Elsbels caus-ed by dry weenter. Eenfact, when waters turn-ed back on you must not showers, but only washes. Terriblee sorry, but thees is Elsbels counceel rules, not hotels. Anybody uses lots of water...'

He made a hanging motion by jerking his right hand by his throat.

'...weel be in beeg troubles and thrown een to preeson. Muchos queekly.'

Pepe had just finished his warning when Ivor Bodie and Bernie Biddle came in through the main entrance carrying Percy Arkwright in his coffin. Widow Arkwright followed behind.

'What yous doos comeeng back with dead mans?' asked Pepe.

'They have no room at the Chapel of Rest,' explained Bodie. 'There has been an outbreak of legionnaire's disease in the area and twenty victims are lying on top of one another in the chapel. Mrs Arkwright quite rightly does not want us to park her husband there in case he catches the disease.'

Farquhar, thinking quickly, immediately decided that he would contact his head office about the need for a vaccine for himself if the outbreak became any more serious.

So Percy was put back on the table tennis table, which greatly annoyed the two Spanish workmen who were at eighteen points all in the deciding game. They played the final points using the coffin as their net, and there was a devil of a row between the two construction workers when the losing player refused to pay up because he claimed that his final smash would have been a winner with a proper net. Instead of that it cannoned off the top of the coffin and walloped widow Arkwright in the eye.

Sydney and Ethel Roper went for a leisurely stroll towards the sea after breakfast, only a mile away. This was on Ethel's insistence because she wanted to get him away from the sight of that show-off Sadie Tompkins, who had come down to the dining room carrying all before her in a tight-fitting white swimsuit. Sydney's eyes had come out so far it had made Ethel hunger for poached eggs on toast.

'What d'you think of my flip flops?' Ethel asked as they walked down Elsbels high street.

Sydney looked at her and gaped. 'Put them away,' he said. 'They don't allow women to go topless here.'

Back at the hotel, Farquhar had been able to account for all but one of his clients. There was no sign of Elvis.

He then noticed a familiar figure coming down for a late breakfast. It was a Harold Wilson lookalike.

James Bedsop had changed his disguise.

It was quite an eventful first day down on the beach for the Wundatours holidaymakers.

Ethel Roper, with a natural skin colour as white as chalk, got so badly sunburned that while lying on the beach in the middle of the afternoon a short-sighted Spanish fisherman mistook her for a giant lobster and threw his net over her.

Sydney Roper did not fare much better. He was splashing merrily along the edge of the water ogling Sadie Tompkins sunbathing on one of the rocks when he slipped on a slimy object. He got up and took a kick at it in anger, and the giant jellyfish, for that is what it was, slithered to the left and retaliated with a sting that within seconds brought Sydney's ankle swelling up to twice its usual size. It was obviously a Spanish jellyfish because the shimmy to the left and then the counter attack was right out of the Real Madrid textbook.

There was no danger of Stanley and Evelyn Blunt getting sunburned. They each wore woolly cardigans despite temperatures nudging the nineties. Evelyn was protected by an ankle-length skirt and sensible sandals, while Stanley wisely wore black socks with his sandals and lemon-coloured shorts, even if he did look – as the Golightly twins succinctly put it in unison – 'a right prat.' The knotted white handkerchief on his head gave a nice finishing touch to this traditional image of the quintessential Englishman abroad.

The Blunts had taken precautions against the sun, but this was no defence against the king-size crab that was so friendly that it attached itself to the big toe on Evelyn's left foot as they walked along the beach. Stanley considered helping the crab to the other foot as well, but Evelyn's screams were drawing too much attention to them. He bent down and got involved in a wrestling match with the crab, and at one stage had it in a half nelson. But as he endeavoured to prise the crab off his wife's big toe, he too was caught by the crustacean. Now there's another novelty.

They were finally freed when the short-sighted Spanish fisherman arrived with a sharp knife and cut them free of the crab after slicing their cardigans to shreds with a few range-finding swipes.

It was very convenient that Sydney Roper and Evelyn Blunt, both limping, were able to share a taxi to the nearest hospital along with Stanley, who was nursing a bleeding thumb. The Elsbels hospital was quarantined because of the outbreak of legionnaire's disease, and they had to make a round trip of one hundred miles for treatment at the nearest alternative medical centre. They had to pay the taxi-driver fifty pounds for the privilege of being bumped almost into unconsciousness by an ancient taxi that, as Sydney so accurately put it, 'would not even be accepted as scrap back 'ome.' As he paid the taxi driver, Sydney showed that he was picking up the lingo. 'Muchos grassyarse,' he said.

Ivor Bodie and Bernie Biddle accompanied Mrs Arkwright to the beach, and they found a nice shady spot down by the rocks for the coffin. Widow

Arkwright had insisted that they bring Percy. 'The fresh air will do him good,' she said.

They persuaded Mrs Arkwright to join them for a cup of tea at the beach restaurant one hundred yards away. By the time they returned the tide had come in, and the coffin was missing. It did not take them long to spot it fifty yards away and heading for North Africa. Neither Bodie nor Biddle could swim, but they were saved by the short-sighted Spanish fisherman who splashed after the coffin with a rope. He first of all lassooed Miss Tompkins, who quite liked the idea of being tied up but not here on the rocks. She freed herself and swam to the coffin and knotted one end of the rope to the handles. The fisherman hauled it back in, and was rewarded with a kiss by Mrs Arkwright. 'This is the most exciting day in my husband's life,' she told him.

The fisherman had been hoping that Miss Tompkins might have given him a similar reward that he would have returned with passion, but she was too busy chatting up Bertie MacConway who had arrived on the beach wearing, apparently, nothing but his kilt.

'Ain't you frightened of getting sunburned?' said Sadie.

'Och, noo,' said Bertie. 'I've got skin like leather from working with my shirt off on Clydeside docks.'

It was less than an hour later when he collapsed with sunstroke, just as Sadie was about to find out why he was nicknamed Big Mac. Bernie Biddle gave him a fireman's lift to the hotel, and then returned to the beach to help Ivor Bodie carry the coffin back in time for their first evening meal at the Grande Elsbels. Mrs

Arkwright was delighted to see him because it rescued her from chapter twenty-seven of Bodie's rambling discourse on the future of package holidays. He was forecasting that Florida would take over from Spain as the main attraction for British holidaymakers, which even Mrs Arkwright with her limited knowledge of geography knew was a crazy notion. 'Blimey,' she said, 'next you'll be saying people will be going to Orstralia for their 'olidays.'

Only the Golightly sisters and the Very Reverend Francis Bigger gave the beach a miss. The twins stayed in the hotel playing ping pong with the two dark and handsome Spanish construction workers, who were about to show the sisters how their drills worked when they were unceremoniously thrown out of the hotel by an irate Pepe. 'I'm sorree you ees beeing peste-red by thees no good mens,' he said to the twins. 'I weel personally see to eet that you are not bother-red agaeen.' He disappeared back to reception before one of the twins was able to reveal that *she* was the one with psychopathic tendencies.

Bigger went off to visit a cardinal and two young priests for a pre-arranged meeting in the grounds of the Church of Elsbels, where he outlined his vision for the religion of the future, with the worship of money as the main message. It was, he claimed, already a movement even more popular than Roman Catholicism. When he asked them to join his crusade in return for a twenty five per cent share of all profits made in Spain, they at first tried to convert *him* and then duffed him up. They gave him a good kicking, crossing themselves as their holy boots went in.

Bigger was then dumped outside the hotel with BEWARE THIS MAN, HE IS THE DEVIL'S MESSENGER written in red paint across the back of his sky-blue cassock. Bigger decided he would spend the rest of the six days on holiday. He realised he was wasting his time trying to spread the word in Spain. They were far too religious, and it made him cross.

There was a strong scent of camomile lotion in the dining room as the Wundatours holidaymakers, most of them scorched by the sun, sat down to their much-awaited evening meal. An excited buzz of chatter passed among them as they realised that Harold Wilson was staying at the hotel. Bedsop, the master of disguise, had already fooled them once today with his appearance as a short-sighted Spanish fisherman while carrying out his special assignment on the beach. Now he had convinced them that he was the former British Prime Minister, and he lectured them about the peseta in their pocket and strongly recommended that their next holidays should be spent on the Isle of Scilly.

It was, inevitably, the Blunts who were first to complain about the meal; first about the slowness of the service, and then about the food itself.

Evelyn, her foot heavily bandaged and wearing one shoe, took only one sip of her tomato soup before moaning. 'This is cold,' she snapped at Stanley. 'Call the head waiter immediately.'

'Yes dear,' Stanley meant to say, but it came out as, 'Call him yourself, you old trout.'

Mrs Blunt put it down to too much sun despite the protection of the handkerchief that was still on his head; he had also, like herself, had a painful experience with the crab and his thumb was bandaged, poor soul. She thought he had been very brave the way he had tackled the crab to try to rescue her. It was reassuring to know that he still cared about her after eighteen years of marriage. 'You do not get crabs acting like that in Guildford,' she had told the doctor at the hospital. 'Our crabs are beautifully dressed and just lie there and let you eat them.'

'Waiter!' Mrs Blunt barked, making everybody at the tables sit up straight as if at school.

Giorgio dragged himself away from the Golighty twins, who were holding a hand each having only just spotted him. They had already nicknamed him 'Giorgious Giorgio.' Which of them was going to get him into bed first? The race was on.

'What do you call this?' said Mrs Blunt, pointing at her soup plate.

'*Si*?' said Giorgio.

'This,' said Mrs Blunt, now tapping the soup plate with her spoon. 'What is this?'

'Ees a plate,' said Giorgio, spreading his arms and hunching his shoulders. 'A soups plate.'

'Not the plate, you stupid Spaniard,' she said. 'What's supposed to be in it?'

'Ees soup,' said Giorgio, wondering how he could get away from the mad woman. 'Ees tomato soup.'

'In Guildford,' said Mrs Blunt, 'tomato soup is served hot. Piping hot. This is like cold water.'

Farquhar came to Giorgio's rescue. 'Cold soup is a speciality of the hotel,' he lied. 'They are famous throughout Elsbels for it.'

'Well I want *hot* tomato soup,' she said firmly. 'Tell them what I want, Stanley.'

'Hot tomato soup, dear,' he meant to say, but it came out as, 'You want that soup poured all over you.'

'Don't take any notice of my husband,' she said. 'He's had too much sun, and was attacked by a crab. Just bring me a plate of *hot* soup. Now.'

'*Si, señora*,' said Giorgio, taking Mrs Blunt's soup plate and rushing to the kitchen. He returned minutes later with the soup steaming from where a contemptuous Floella had placed it on the hot plate. As he bent to place it on the table, Giorgio tripped over Mrs Blunt's outstretched bandaged foot. She first of all screamed because of the pain in her foot, and then shrieked again as a plateful of steaming hot tomato soup was deposited in her lap.

The incident caused a bit of an atmosphere in the dining room, and it plunged into one of almost open revolt twenty minutes later when Pepe was forced to make an announcement. 'On behalf of Elsbels hotel I have to make apologees to all you loverlee residents and Señor Farque,' he said. 'You were goings to heats beautifuls roast-ed beefs, but eet has been taken by hotel guard dog wheech I have given good keek up bumsides. Muchos sorrees.'

Sydney Roper, his stung, swollen foot throbbing inside its bandage, summed up the feelings of the entire party. 'We've been here almost two days and ain't had any decent grub yet,' he said. 'Even bleeding prisoners get three square meals a day.'

A perspiring Floella came into the dining room from the kitchen. 'I soree ees very very,' she said. 'I was beefs going to cook for tonight's deener, but my husband daft he forgets horder eet. One ofs thees days he heads hee's forgets.'

Pepe pushed his wife out of the dining room, screaming away at her in Spanish.

Once again Farquhar led his protesting party to the Union Jack for bangers and mash, and after they had been fed and had supped a drink or three they began to relax and laugh about the day's adventures, the way only true Brits could. It was Harold Wilson who led them on a sing song, with a very passable imitation of Elvis Presley.

Mrs Arkwright persuaded Bodie and Biddle to bring the coffin with them, and it was given a place of honour on the bar. Everybody was moved to tears when Mrs Arkwright sang, 'My old man said follow the van'.

An enjoyable evening ended with Percy, in his coffin, of course, taking part in a conga all the way back to the hotel. Mrs Arkwright said that Percy had not enjoyed himself so much in years.

Only the Golightly sisters were missing from the impromptu party at the Union Jack. They were searching through the hotel for 'Giorgious Giorgio,' who had hidden himself away. He spent the night tucked out of sight in the empty swimming pool. After his exhausting experience the previous night with Sadie Tompkins, he did not have the energy to be singled out... and certainly not twinned.

Elsbels, Friday

Dear Mum,
Having a nice time. Wish you were here. We have taken all the precautions you recommended, and are putting on lots of sun protection cream and keeping our legs crossed. There are several eligible bachelors in our hotel, and we are making polite conversation with them in the hope that it might lead to a gentle romance. Thinking of you. Love **Gladys** xxx and **Gladys** xxx

Mrs T. Golightly,
27 Rubberduck Avenue,
Coventry,
Warwickshire,
England.

4

ELSBELS, FRIDAY 2 JUNE 1973

It was the first organised excursion day of the Wundatours holiday, and Stuart Farquhar looked forward to it with as much enthusiasm as he would a visit to the dentist for root canal treatment. In fact he would have chosen the dentist's drill rather than the ordeal of what was billed in the brochure as 'an olé 'olé day experience'. This was to be a day devoted to the traditional Spanish way of life, with a visit to a pearl factory, a bull fight and an evening barbecue on the agenda.

The day got off to a bad start, although Farquhar had the feeling that this was going to be as good as it got. Floella, who was about as expert a cook as Douglas Bader was a ballroom dancer, burned the porridge and managed to make the bacon runny, the fried eggs crispy and the sausages unrecognisable.

Pepe did not help the early-morning mood when revealing that toast would be 'hextra'. The fact that Floella had burned it to a cinder made no difference. 'Eet ees how we always have our toast in Elsbels,' said Pepe. 'Our bread, eet ees, how you Eengleesh say, "the toast of the town."'

It was the Blunts, firmly established as the lead moaners, who were the first to complain. 'This is quite inedible, waiter,' said Mrs Blunt to Giorgio. 'It is the sort of food that we would feed to our dogs in Guildford.'

Giorgio took this to be a compliment. 'Muchos sank yous,' he said, bowing and beaming. 'I tell chef you likes food so muchos that you geev it to your dogs.'

Mrs Blunt crooked a finger at Farquhar, sitting across the dining room. As he made his reluctant way towards the moaning bitch he was running a parade of ready-made company excuses through his mind in preparation for the predictable complaint coming his way.

'Listen, my man,' said Mrs Blunt. 'This food is an absolute disgrace. It distinctly said in the Wundatours brochure that there was a *cordon bleu* chef in residence at the hotel. Tell him what it said in the brochure, Stanley.'

'I reserve all rights against you,' said Stanley, mindful of the legal smallprint, 'in as much as and pursuant to the Fair Trade Act of 1971 and notwithstanding that the editor's decision is final and binding in all matters and that no employees or relatives may participate, and witnessed herewith by those present and cognizant of the party of the third part, it is my prerequisite duty under oath and subsequent to all other clauses that I, Stanley Clement Blunt, do point out with no cause or just impediment that the Wundatours brochure did allegedly state that there would be a *cordon bleu* chef in residence.'

Farquhar was shuffling through all possible responses while Blunt waffled away, and finally settled for his own personal escape plan: WHEN IN DOUBT, FAINT. He collapsed to the floor, making sure that he cushioned his fall on Mrs Blunt's bandaged foot. She screamed and the other diners recoiled in shock.

Ivor Bodie and Bernie Biddle, perhaps a little too dramatically, carried Farquhar back shoulder high at funereal pace to his table and sat him on his seat. A panicking Giorgio summoned Pepe, who brought Farquhar round with an expertly aimed jug of cold water.

'Señor Farque does thees everry year,' Pepe explained. 'I tells heem he should wear sombrero because sun it ees too hot for heem and drive heem loco. But he no leessen.'

Farquhar gave a performance worthy of an Oscar nomination as he pretended to wonder where he was and what had happened. But there was no escaping the Blunts.

'As I was saying,' said Mrs Blunt, 'there is supposed to be a *cordon bleu* chef in residence.'

'What d'you say to that, hotel manager?' he said to Pepe weakly, knowing when he was beaten.

'I no understand why yous asks theese question,' said Pepe. 'My wifes she ees recognis-ed as best cook in whole of Elsbels. Spanish hotel guide book says she *cordon bleu* standard. It says in book she should be cordoned off because she geev hotel guests muchos blues.'

Farquhar was just about to feign another fainting performance when Giorgio shouted out the good news that the excursion coach had arrived. The bad news was that it was the same old bus that had broken down on the way from the airport.

In the background a Max Bygraves lookalike, taking the place of Harold Wilson, held the rapt attention of the other holidaymakers. 'I wanna tell you a story,' he said, and then proceeded to tell them the history of Fleet Street. Bedsop had got his Max Bygraves mixed up with Max Beaverbrook.

Farquhar went slowly up to his room and got his sombrero out of the wardrobe, trying to ignore the fact that he was looking into the adjoining room where the Very Reverend Francis Biddle was taking a swig from his Bible.

Perhaps, Farquhar thought, Pepe was right. Maybe too much sun *was* sending him loco.

Mrs Arkwright was persuaded to leave Percy behind on the table tennis table. 'A rest will do him the world of good,' she was assured by Ivor Bodie. 'I do not think the Spaniards would take kindly to us taking a coffin into the bull ring.'

Pedro, the coach driver, greeted each passenger with a gap-toothed grin. 'Steek your facking teeps,' he said to each of them, and he was still empty handed by the time they had all sat down. Perhaps Pepe was right when he advised that he should try hinting at a tip at the end rather than the beginning of the journey, but as he rarely got to the scheduled end in this ancient coach he liked to try to get in early.

There were grumbles about the coach being the wreck that had let them down on their arrival, but the Max Bygraves lookalike cheered everybody up by leading them in a sing-along. Only the Golightly sisters declined to join in. They were both still sulking because, so far, they had not landed 'Giorgious Giorgio'.

The bone shaker of a coach rattled its way back up

the mountain road and free-wheeled down the other side to the Elsbels pearl factory. Farquhar, addressing the tour party from beneath his huge sombrero, explained that there would be a buffet served at the rear of the factory after they had enjoyed the riveting sight of watching the workers manufacturing the pearls.

'I can't bleedin' wait,' said Sydney Roper. 'I'm sure it will be very nearly as exciting as watching fingernails being cut.'

As it turned out, it was much more exciting. Dear old Mrs Arkwright appeared to get a little muddled because a buffet had been mentioned. It was quite understandable that she thought the pearls were *petit fours* and she was spotted swallowing them. There was quite an altercation when the manager of the factory accused her of stealing the pearls, and Farquhar had to pay the equivalent of fifty pounds to appease him. It was estimated that Mrs Arkwright was walking around with enough pearls for a necklace inside her.

'She'll drop one, pearl one in the loo tonight,' said Sadie Tompkins, who was being escorted on the tour by Bertie MacConway. This was much to the hidden anger of Sydney Roper, who had paid for Sadie's holiday but was getting none of the perks.

There was then a violent confrontation in the pearl purchasing shop, a room that led from the factory to the buffet bar as a craftily situated tourist trap. Sadie Tompkins and Ethel Roper had each simultaneously picked up the same double string of pearls from the counter, and then started a tug of war.

'I saw them first,' said Ethel through clenched teeth.

'But I picked them up first,' said Sadie, tugging at her end.

As they tried to wrench the pearls from each other the string snapped, and fifty imitation pearls were suddenly rolling around the marble floor. The Very Reverend Bigger, already unsteady on his feet because he had drunk the contents of his Bible, trod on one and went skidding into a glass cabinet that shattered.

The factory manager, rushing in to see what was happening, found his feet giving away under him and he sailed head first into Bertie MacConway, who instinctively retaliated with a Glasgie kiss. He butted the manager straight between the eyes and sent him backwards into the remains of the cabinet half destroyed by Bigger.

When he came round, the manager agreed not to press charges after Farquhar had guaranteed to pay instant damages of five hundred pounds that he hoped would be covered by the Wundatours insurance. He knew he would have to be really imaginative with his report, and decided to do his best to make it sound like something out of Pearl Harbor.

By the time Farquhar got to the buffet bar, every morsel had been eaten by his ravenous party. Who, he thought, would be a bloody courier. In future, he would remember to eat first, act later. That was his one pearl of wisdom for the day.

Next stop, the Elsbels bullring. It was not quite what the Golightly sisters had been expecting. They had been to the Bullring in Birmingham, and had been prepared for a shopping spree. As the *corrida*[1] began with the grand entry procession of the *cuadrillas*[2] led by the mounted *alguaciles*[3], the twins watched in open-mouthed wonder as one of the oldest and most spectacular of all sporting opening ceremonies unfolded before their eyes. It was, they thought at an identical moment, one of the most beautiful sights they had ever seen, and they became instant bull fighting fans. The matadors followed in their short jackets, waistcoats, and knee-length, skintight trousers of silk and satin, richly embroidered in gold and silver silk. Draped over their shoulders were satin dress capes, and they wore coral-pink heavy silk stockings, flat heelless black slippers, and *monteras*[4] made of tiny black silk chenille balls hand sewn in personalised designs on heavy buckram. They were accompanied by their *banderilleros*[5] who were adorned in similar colourful garments, lacking only the gold embroidery which is exclusive to matadors. The mounted picadors, with their broad-rimmed, low-crowned beige hats and ornate hip-to-ankle protective armour, added to the spectacle that had the audience, the Golightly sisters in particular, spellbound.

The first matador came into the arena and performed his initial passes, working gracefully and bravely close to the horns. The cries of *olé* from the crowd every time

[1]*Corrida:* The bullfight event, the full Spanish name being *corrida de toros,* from the Latin *currere,* "to run," and *taurus,* "bull."
[2]*Cuadrillas*: the matador's troupes, or assistants.
[3]*Alguaciles*: mounted assistants (bailiffs in 16th Century costume).
[4]*Monteras*: matadors' hats.
[5]*Banderilleros*: assistants on foot, who also work with the cape and place the *banderillas* (staves) into the bulls.

he made a pass brought the Golightly twins leaping to their feet in excitement. Why, the twins wondered as they watched the spectacle, was there so much controversy about bull fighting. The bull was unharmed apart from being made perhaps a little dizzy as he twisted and turned trying to butt the swirling cape. During this mesmerising cape work, a bugle sounded to signal the entrance of the picadors and the beginning of the first three acts building up to the kill. Now the actual bull fighting had begun, and as the first of the picador's lances sank into the bull at the junction of the neck and shoulder blades, the Golightly sisters fainted, Gladys One a second ahead of Gladys Two. Their love affair with bull fighting was at an end.

The faces of the watching Wundatours holidaymakers turned green as they witnessed in sickened silence their first ever bull being put to the sword. Farquhar, the only one of the group who had been before, had his face hidden inside his sombrero. He had learned long ago that he had as much affinity with bull fighting as El Cordobes had with Morris dancing.

Evelyn Blunt led the protests. 'This is a disgrace,' she yelled, her voice booming around the bullring. 'Tell them Stanley.'

For once, Stanley agreed. 'Shame on you all,' he shouted, not knowing nor caring that he looked a complete twit with shirt and braces, blue shorts, black socks and sandals and, of course, the knotted handkerchief on his head.

A proud Spaniard in the row in front stood up ready

to defend his nation's national spectacle.

'No, sir, shame on *you*,' he said in perfect English. 'You are a guest in our country, and it is appalling manners to behave as you are. How would you like it if I suddenly started bawling out during a Test match at Lord's?'

'But nobody dies in cricket,' said Stanley.

'Only the spectators from boredom,' said the Spaniard. 'I, sir, have seen Geoffrey Boycott bat.'

That stumped Stanley. 'Come on, dear,' he said to Evelyn, 'we're getting out of here. We're not watching any more of this barbarity.'

All the tour party stood up to leave apart from Bertie MacConway. 'I've paid good money tae see this,' he said, 'and I'm going tae get my moneys worth.' He joined them at the coach an hour later, unable to stomach any more of the blood letting. 'Och,' he said, 'it must have been like that at Bannockburn.'

Amazingly, the coach got them to the barbecue almost on time, well, just an hour late which for Pedro was as good as he could get. Ivor Bodie complained that his funeral cars moved faster on the way to the cemetary. They had assumed that the barbecue was exclusive to them, and so were rather surprised to find they were joining four hundred other sun-scorched, bored, ripped-off package holidaymakers from Britain. There were lashings of red and white Spanish plonk, much of it being poured over shirt and blouse fronts as half-cut Brits tried to come to grips with traditional long-stemmed containers that made every mouthful a challenge. Sadly, there were also lashings of rain. No sooner had the Wundatours party sat down at the long trestle tables packed tightly together in a cinema car park than the heavens opened. It bucketed down and their chickens floated in their baskets and their chips were so soggy that they were better sucked than chewed. A trio of guitarists accompanied a Flamenco dancer, who splashed through the puddles on the tables until giving way to a rather drunk Bertie MacConway who insisted on doing the Highland Fling with the Flamenco dancer's rose between his teeth. He only let her get on with her solo act when she attacked up his kilt with her snapping castanets to a roar of encouragement from the other tourists, who were now so drunk they had forgotten what a miserable time they were having.

The guitarists and the Flamenco dancer retreated for the night when they realised they could not compete with the Max Bygraves lookalike. The traditional Spanish evening had given way to a good old British knees-up. Max was standing on the table leading a sing-along, and he had most success with 'April Showers', 'Raindrops Keep Falling on My Head' and a particularly spirited version of 'The Rain in Spain', during which Sydney Roper, bandaged foot and all, danced a tango on the table with Sadie Tompkins.

This did not go down too well with Ethel Roper, and the barbecue ended with she and Sadie rolling on the muddy ground pulling at each other's hair. They were dragged apart by a very drunk Very Reverend Francis Bigger, who made the sign of the cross and forgave them both. He whispered to Sadie that she could come to his room and make a full confession any time she felt like it. Sadie reacted by kneeing him in the cassock.

The rain storm had knocked out all the lights on the barbecue site, and everybody suddenly started to give Bigger a wide berth. It was only some time later that he discovered that the BEWARE THIS MAN, HE IS THE DEVIL'S MESSENGER warning on the back of his sky-blue cassock had been written in luminous red paint.

The Wundatours party returned dripping wet to their coach to find no sign of Pedro, the driver. After an hour, it was decided that Bernie Biddle should drive the coach back to the Grande Elsbels. He was an experienced hearse driver, and reluctantly agreed to take on the challenge provided somebody else concentrated on the navigation.

With a loud grating of gears, the coach started off on its journey at the funereal pace to which Biddle was accustomed. He had never driven a vehicle more than fifteen miles an hour in his life. Stanley Blunt acted as navigator, and kept jumping out and running ahead to look at signposts.

Apart from the minor problem that he kept forgetting he should have been driving on the right side of the road, Biddle made good progress until they started the mountain climb where the coach had broken down on their first day. They were still a mile away from the top before the downward run to the hotel and the coach was shuddering and shaking as it groaned along at five miles an hour. Everybody but Biddle had their eyes shut tight rather than glance out to the deep shadows either side picked out in the dancing yellow headlights of the coach. The shadows hid sheer drops to the rocks hundreds of feet below. The Very Reverend Bigger was praying aloud for them all as they wondered if this coach would become their hearse.

It was just looking and sounding as if the gasping coach was not going to make it when Biddle had a brain wave. He told them all to get off the coach, and when he started up again he found that it chugged comfortably to the top of the mountain road. Biddle then got out and returned to meet the party on their way up towards the coach. He carried Mrs Arkwright on his broad shoulders, and helped Stanley Blunt assist his limping wife on the climb. Bertie MacConway was supporting the hobbling Sydney Roper and the Golightly sisters took on the job of keeping the warring Sadie Tompkins and Ethel Roper apart. The Max Bygraves clone was doing his best to keep up their spirits, but his sing-along had become a solo as he belted out 'Climb Every Mountain' from *The Sound of Music*.

Meanwhile, Pedro the driver had woken up on the back seat of the coach where he had been stretched out asleep. He had no recollection of getting to the top of the mountain road, and wondered whether he had been drinking. The Wundatours party had just got to within fifty yards of the coach when it suddenly coughed into life and chugged off out of sight and down the mountain road, with Pedro cursing that once again he had received no facking tips. One reasonable tip was that he should avoid any members of the Wundatours party for the forseeable future.

It was two hours later when the exhausted holidaymakers

returned to the Grande Elsbels. They were astonished to find it floodlit, and with a hammering and drilling racket going on that made it sound like a car breaker's yard. The hotel was crawling with workers.

Farquhar immediately sorted out Pepe, who was in the kitchen with his wife stacking away a mountainous supply of fresh food.

'What the hell's going on?' he said. 'What are all these workmen doing all over the hotel?'

'Hah, Señor Farque,' said Pepe, 'we are working to get hotel sheep shape, as it should be for your holiday clients.'

'But why now?' asked Farquhar, spreading his arms. 'Why in the middle of the night?'

'Ees the only time all mens availables,' explained Pepe. 'Tomorrow when you wakes ups you finds hotel all finished and splendeed.'

'But nobody will be able to sleep with this racket,' protested Farquhar.

'I theenks you wrong, Señor Farque,' said Pepe, pointing out into the hotel lounge where the worn out members of his tour party were stretched out on armchairs and sofas fast asleep.

Farquhar shrugged and prepared to go to bed. 'Where has all this food come from?' he asked Floella as he walked to the door.

'Thees has deliver-ed been today,' said Floella. 'We need food lots for our guests new.'

'What new guests?' asked Farquhar, stifling a yawn.

'Another party joins us tomorrow,' said Pepe. 'Vundatours of Hamburg.'

Elsbels, Friday

Dear Monica,
Having a nice time, wish you were here. Very disappointed that there is not a single excursion to a graveyard, and I have yet to see a Spanish funeral. At least there are no bloody foreigners in our hotel apart from the Spanish staff. We flew out here on Betty Grable which reminded me of all the good times in the war. Hope you have plenty of clients waiting for me on my return. Your loving husband, **Ivor Bodie** xxx

Mrs Monica Bodie,

Bodie's Funeral Home,

Deadend Crescent,

Isleworth,

Middlesex,

Good old England.

5

ELSBELS, SATURDAY 3 JUNE 1973

THE German invasion started at 1200 hours. A luxury air conditioned Mercedes-engined coach purred through the gates of the Grande Elsbels exactly on schedule. On board were fifty passengers from Hamburg, forty of them holidaymakers and the rest specialist staff to look after their every need. They had brought with them their own chefs, waiters, maids and porters.

By 1400 hours they were comfortably ensconced in their double rooms, all with sea views, in the suddenly opened west wing of the hotel, and they had been fed a beautifully prepared four-course meal, with Floella allowed in the kitchen only to wash up the dishes. By 1430 hours they were camped under sun umbrellas round the hotel pool that had been filled with water that morning. There was not a workman in sight, and everything was in perfect working order. The sun shone down from a clear blue sky, and Marlene Dietrich records were being played over the Tannoy.

'*Alles ist wunderschön*,' Vundatours öbergross courier Helmut Schmartarsch told a bowing and scraping Pepe, who stood to earn ten times as much from the German tourists as from the British. They expected the best and paid the best prices in return, while Pepe found that the British were always moaning and groaning and wanted something for nothing.

Only that morning they had objected to him charging 'hextra' for the marmalade, while the so efficient and organised Germans had arrived with their own supply along with enough sauerkraut, liverwürst and frankfurters to last them a month.

The British holidaymakers had no knowledge of the new arrivals, Farquhar choosing not to tell them for fear that it would make their moods of depression even deeper. He had enough problems keeping them happy without telling them they were about to be invaded by what Sydney Roper, for instance, would call 'a crowd of Krauts.'

After another burnt offering of a breakfast from Floella, the British Wundatours party had been whisked off to tour a local tanning factory where they parted with more of their pesetas for simulated leather and suede bags, purses and coats that they could have got at half the price in any London market.

An apparent misunderstanding led to another hair-pulling duel between Ethel Roper and Sadie Tompkins. Ethel later insisted that when she said 'look at that scraggy old bag' she was referring to a scuffed, second-hand leather handbag that was for sale. Sadie preferred to think otherwise, and they had to be separated as they rolled around in the leather showroom. Bertie MacConway found it quite a turn-on, and put in a special order to have a kilt made of simulated leather and to include tartan lining so that he could show off his clan when doing the Highland Fling.

The Golightly sisters bought identical pairs of imitation leather trousers one minute after each other, and the shop assistant who served them thought that she was experiencing a powerful case of *déjà vu*. She then sold them each what was described as a 'genuine' soft-leather cardigan and a suede sweater which the sisters said were the perfect twin set. They were not to know that it was fake material, and the assistant was not to know that the twins were paying with counterfeit money that Mrs Arkwright had given to them in return for their travellers' cheques.

Mrs Arkwright, proudly showing off the new string of pearls adorning her neck, caused another ruckus when she was spotted walking out of the shop wearing three suede coats and carrying two leather handbags over each arm. The shop manager reluctantly accepted the story that she was old and forgetful, but Farquhar was beginning to harbour doubts about the grieving widow. He was wondering if perhaps she was a queen kleptomaniac, a suspicion that strengthened when he saw her putting the empty teacup and saucer into her bag after they had stopped off for a snack lunch in the leather factory cafeteria.

Her deceased husband had been barred from entering the factory because the manager, quite unreasonably, had claimed it would be bad for business to have a coffin being carried around his showroom. Ivor Bodie was most indignant, and pointed out that in his view, admittedly fairly biased, the sight of a coffin being borne shoulder high was one of the most beautiful sights to be seen and would draw rather than deter customers. But the manager was dead against it.

Bodie and Bernie Biddle took turns 'body sitting'

outside the showroom so that Mrs Arkwright could do her shopping, or rather shoplifting. She remembered to take something for Percy, take being the operative word. She lifted a very nice leather belt for him that would help keep his trousers up now that he was likely to experience a serious weight loss.

Percy Arkwright had almost been one of London's greatest forgers, and would have had no peers if he had been able to spell properly. He even forged his own death curtificate, and only his widow knew that just about every piece of paper she possessed, including her marrige curtificate, pissport, driving lisense, holliday vouchers and Spinish and Englesh currency, were as false as Ivor Bodie's clattering teeth but not quite so detectable.

The Very Reverend Francis Bigger managed to sell a leather-bound Bible to the factory manager, having convinced him that it was a one-off made from the skin of the Yeti. The manager knew that a man of the cloth would never have lied to him, but how was he to know that the cloth that Bigger wore was as fake as the leather on the Bible and much of the leather in the factory showroom.

Stanley Blunt bought a leather mask that he was going to slip over his wife's face in bed at night to try to silence her snoring, and Sydney Roper purchased a leather thonged whip that he explained to Ethel he would be giving to Lester Piggott when in truth he was planning to use it in his next session with 'Insatiable' Sadie. They liked to play horse and jockey, and it was his turn for a ride. He just hoped he was going to be allowed at least one jump on the holiday that he had orginally planned as a wife-free zone.

Bedsop had now made an appearance as Rolf Harris, and he confused the assistant by asking for a leather billycan to dip in his billabong. They were asked to kindly leave the premises when Rolf started splashing paint all over the wall while singing 'Tie Me Kangaroo Down Sport.'

Farquhar, wanting to delay as long as possible the news that the Wundatours party no longer had exclusive use of the Grande Elsbels facilities, next led them down to the harbour for a boat excursion that was included in the price of the package holiday. The spirits of the tourists – perspiring in their newly acquired simulated leather accessories – rose when they saw the luxury yachts moored in the exclusive Elsbels marina, but they sank just as quickly when they were ushered aboard an old rust bucket that looked about as seaworthy as a colander.

'It distinctly said in the brochure,' moaned Mrs Blunt to Farquhar, 'that this holiday included a trip aboard a luxury yacht. Tell him, Stanley, that this is not what counts as luxury in Guildford.'

'Yes dear,' Stanley meant to say, but it came out as, 'I hope you fall over the side and get gobbled up by a shark, you old crab.'

Evelyn Blunt turned to Farquhar. 'You see,' she said, 'the shock of being aboard this apology of a boat has made him delirious.'

She straightened the knotted handkerchief on her husband's head, and loosened the woollen scarf around his neck. 'Pull yourself together, Stanley,' she ordered. 'Remember, you're representing Guildford.'

The captain was a gnarled old sea dog whose weather-beaten skin was the same rust-coloured red as his boat, and he looked as much of a tramp as his vessel. The half-empty rum bottle sticking out of the waistband on his bell bottom trousers did not fill his passengers with confidence. 'Shenorsh, shenorash and lovelys shenoritash,' he shouted, flashing a toothless leer at the Golightly sisters and Sadie Tompkins, 'welcomesh haboard the...'

'Marie Celeste,' said Sydney Roper.

'...Shanta Maria. I am your capitansh Alfredo Gonzalesh. We weelsh shailsh haround the beautifulsh port of Elshbelsh and I weelsh point out placesh of heestoricalsh eenterestsh. Firstsh, I would asksh you pleashesh to all movesh into the meedle of the boat to helps the balancesh.'

This meant that Ethel Roper had to reluctantly get out of the lifeboat and move with the rest of the party to the centre of what appeared to be a botched together mixture of a sailing yacht and tug, which is exactly what it was. In the car trade it would have been called a cut-and-shut.

Gonzales had been a tug captain who, while drunk as a skunk at the wheel, collided with a yacht in this very harbour twenty years earlier. During his two-year ban from skippering anything that moved on water, he had salvaged the two vessels and welded the least damaged bits together.

It was now neither a sailing yacht nor a tug, more of

a yug. Or, as most passengers called it on first sight, a yuk.

The sun-dappled Mediterranean was as serene and as still as a millpond, but the Santa Maria had not gone one hundred yards from the mooring point before half the party were throwing up over the side of a boat that was pitching and rolling like a raft in a storm. It might perhaps have had something to do with the fact that it was being driven by a propeller that had been salvaged from an ocean liner.

'Here on your rightsh,' slurred Gonzales, 'eesh the famous harbour of Elshbelsh where in feefteen eighty eightsh the magnifico Spaneesh Armada sheenks the pirate Franceesh Drakesh fleetsh of eenvading Eenglish sheeps.'

He had clearly read a different history book to that available in English schools.

'And here on your leftsh,' said Gonzales, as the Santa Maria flipped around to face the way she had come, 'eesh the famous harbour of Elshbelsh where in feefteen eighty eightsh the magnifico Spaneesh Armada sheenks the pirate Franceesh Drakesh fleetsh of eenvading Eenglish sheeps.'

Behind him, nobody was taking any notice of the history lesson. They were too busy trying to keep themselves upright and their food down.

The Golightly sisters, their green faces matching nicely with their fake leather and suede twin sets, were hanging on to each other like human life belts.

'What the facking hell is this maniac trying to do to us?' started Gladys One.

'Drown us on what's supposed to be a facking pleasure trip?' finished Gladys Two.

The Very Reverend Francis Bigger was clinging to the mast with one hand and was holding his coat hanger-size cross aloft with the other and pointing it towards the sea. He was trying to part the waves so that he could walk back to dry land. 'Verily, verily and thrice verily,' he said, 'if I survive this voyage I will personally chop Señor Gonzales into extremely small slices with his ruddy rudder. He will be a-m-a-z-e-d at what I will do to him, missus.'

Farquhar, trying to find good news where only bad news existed, thought to himself that at least this had stopped Mrs Blunt moaning. She was too busy being seasick to speak. Stanley Blunt was tempted to take the opportunity to push her over the side, but did not have the strength because he, too, was reaching over the side and holding a full kit inspection. Farquhar was alongside them in similar straits while making a mental note to suggest to head office that this excursion should possibly be dropped from the tour agenda.

The Rolf Harris lookalike was endeavouring to stick his didgeridoo up the captain's aft, but even using Jake the Peg's third leg he was still unable to keep on his feet long enough to get a good thrust.

Bodie and Biddle were having a Dickens of a job keeping Percy's coffin aloft on their shoulders. They dare not put him down for fear that he would be washed overboard as the boat bucked and reared as if rounding the Cape of Good Hope in a hurricane. Bodie was trying to remember the words for a burial at sea, and hoping that it would not need to be a dual ceremony because Mrs Arkwright had wrapped herself around her husband's coffin. 'If we're going,' she said, 'we're going together.'

'Ahead of ush,' said the extremely drunk Captain Gonzales as the boat spun one hundred and eighty degrees in a whirlpool of its own making, 'eesh the famous harbour of Elshbelsh where in feefteen eighty eightsh the magnifico Spaneesh Armada sheenks the pirate Franceesh Drakesh fleetsh of eenvading Eenglish sheeps.'

It was bookmaker Sydney Roper, taking time off from offering odds of two to one that they would sink before leaving the harbour, who claimed the Fletcher Christian role and led the mutiny aimed at wresting control of the boat from the unhinged captain.

'I've 'ad enough of this,' he shouted to Bertie MacConway, who was the least affected by the lurchings of the boat because of his experience as a former Aberdeen trawlerman. 'Let's get that mad man off the wheel and this bucket back to the marina.'

Using the whip that he had bought at the leather factory, Roper advanced on Captain Gonzales at the prow of the boat. He cracked the whip at Gonzales as if he were a lion tamer, and the crazy captain reacted by leaping overboard and swimming the hundred yards back to shore leaving the 'loco Eengleesh' to their fate.

MacConway switched off the boat's engine, and the giant, churning propeller that was causing all the problems. Now the Santa Maria was becalmed, much to the relief of all on board. She was brought slowly back to her moorings by the Rolf Harris lookalike using his middle leg as if he was a gondolier.

The Very Reverend Francis Bigger, holding his cross in his hand like a cudgel, headed the posse searching for Captain Gonzales as they climbed ashore on wobbly legs. But they missed him as he disappeared into the distance driven by his getaway driver Pedro in the familiar old bus. Gonzales and Pedro were partners in the tourist transport business, and Wundatours were their only clients.

On their return to the hotel, the British holidaymakers were pleasantly surprised to be told that the water was at last in the pool. That was the good news. The bad news was that they could not see the pool for sunbathing, swimming, exercising, posing, splashing, towelling, diving Germans.

'We've been facking well invaded...' started Gladys Golightly One.

'By Germans,' finished Gladys Golightly Two.

Mrs Blunt trapped the forlorn Farquhar by the balustrades; most painful. 'What are you going to do about these awful foreigners?' she said, pointing a finger in the direction of the pool. 'We cannot get near the pool for German bodies.'

'They are as entitled to use the pool facilities as you or any other resident,' said Farquhar, having decided not to take up the fainting option. 'It is a case, I am afraid, of first come first served.'

'But we were here first,' protested Mrs Blunt, who could not swim a stroke but was always looking to make waves. 'We have been here for what seems like a year without dipping a toe in the pool. Now the water's in at last and we can't get near it.'

She wanted to call Stanley in for one of his blistering contributions, but he was busy trying to soothe widow Arkwright who was having hysterics in the table tennis room. It appeared that somebody had kidnapped Percy. He had been placed back on the table tennis table after they had returned from the traumatic voyage around the harbour. Bodie and Biddle had taken her for a pot of tea, and both Percy and the coffin were now missing. The confused Mrs Arkwright wondered at first whether he could have forged his disappearance, but she had to remind herself that her husband really was dead and that his days as the Great Deceiver were over. So where on earth had he got to?

The Rolf Harris lookalike decided there was only one man who could solve the mystery. Bedsop slipped into the cloakroom and removed his beard and glasses and stuck on a small black moustache and instantly became Hercule Poirot. He was not too hot on a Belgian accent, so he settled for his Maurice Chevalier impersonation. The straw boater and walking cane gave that extra little touch, but he found it a devil of a job getting spats to fit on to his sandals.

Bedsop summoned Pepe, Floella and Giorgio to the room from where the coffin had disappeared. 'Where were you, monsieur, at five or six or seven when the body was stolen?' he asked a perspiring Pepe, who thought the last he had seen of the coffin was when it accompanied the widow on the trip to the leather factory. He was so overworked that it was affecting his memory, and he could not recall what had happened just five minutes ago let alone the five hours since the Wundatours party had left on their excursion.

'I ees workings in receptions all day making sure the new guests they ees happys,' he said. 'I knows nuthings about bodee missing until just now when I hears Mrs Harkwright's screams. She scares flipping sheets out of me.'

Poirot noticed the pearls of perspiration on his brow, which was a sure sign of guilt. He would watch him closely.

'And you, madam,' he said to Floella, 'can you account for your movements?'

'I verry regular ees,' said Floella. 'It ees all to do with my muchos fruit diet. I never toilet mees. But what thees has to do with bodee missing?'

'Not bowel movements, madam,' said Poirot sharply. 'Where were you when the kidnap occured? You should remember it well.'

'I know not where I was,' said Floella, 'because I know not whens disappeared body.'

A likely story, thought Poirot. He could see just by looking at her that she was obviously an accomplice in league with the hotel manager. He noticed the familiar way in which they looked at each other and guessed that they were working together. They had not fooled him. He would pick his moment to unmask them as the masterminds behind the kidnapping.

He now looked directly at Giorgio, who was smiling over his shoulder in the direction of the Golightly sisters

1. Hotel manager Pepe Ripoffola (Peter Butterworth, extreme right) welcomes the British tourists to Elsbels at the start of their holiday from hell. *BFI Stills*

2. Bertie 'Big Mac' MacConway (Jimmy Logan, right) threatens Stuart Farquha (Kenneth Williams) with a bunch of 'Macfives'. *BFI Stills*

3. Eustance Tuttle (Charles Hawtrey), reappearing in the book as private dick James Bedsop, gets some motherly advice. *BFI Stills*

4. Vic Flange (Sidney James), reappearing in the book as Sydney Roper, drinks in the 'twin peak' sights. *BFI Stills*

5. The Blunts (Kenneth Connor and June Whitfield) are on the warpath, leaving courier Stuart Farquhar feeling in need of a holiday. *BFI Stills*

7. Prison cell feasting with Vic Flange (Sidney James), Sadie Tompkins (Barbara Windsor) and Stuart Farquhar (Kenneth Williams).

8. Brother Bernard (Bernard Bresslaw), reappearing in the book as the undertaker Bernie Biddle, and Brother Martin (Derek Francis, right) get cross on holiday.
BFI Stills

9. The excitable Eustance Tuttle (Charles Hawtrey) is feeling fruity in the film.
BFI Stills

10. Vic Flange (Sidney James) suggests a little roll to his wife Cora (Joan Sims). *BFI Stills*

11. Hotel manager Pepe Ripoffola (Peter Butterworth) and his wife Floella (Hattie Jacques) are mixing it in the kitchen. *BFI Stills*

12. It's a teasing time for Eustance Tuttle (Charles Hawtrey) as he carries on abroad.

blowing him kisses from the hotel lounge.

'Who are you, monsieur?' he asked Giorgio, watching him blow kisses back to the twins. 'You obviously sank 'eavens for little girls.' He took another look at the Golightly sisters and corrected himself. 'You obviously sank 'eavens for *big* girls.'

'I Giorgio,' he said, half bowing. 'Head waiter.'

'When did you last see the body?'

'*Si*?'

'The body, monsieur,' Poirot said, getting impatient. 'When and where did you last see it.'

'Hah, bodee,' said Giorgio. 'Eet here on table when new guests arrives. Then, poof. Gone. Vamoose.'

'Just like that,' said Bedsop, accidentally slipping into the Tommy Cooper impression that he did so well.

He quickly got back into character as Poirot. 'I do not want any of you leaving the hotel until my investigation is over,' he said, and he then indicated Pepe with a finger. 'You, bring the man in charge of the new guests here to me immediately. And remember, every little breeze seems to whisper Louise. So I want to interview also this Louise and Gigi, who is no longer the little girl I once knew.'

'This is all I need,' thought Pepe to himself as he went to fetch Herr Schmartarsch. 'A loco detective.'

The rest of the British holidaymakers were hunting through the hotel for the coffin. Bodie and Biddle led the search party. They felt particularly guilty because the coffin and its occupier were their responsibility. Mrs Arkwright had generously paid them – in wads of brand new notes – to come out to Elsbels to look after her late husband, not to enjoy a holiday. But both had got into the holiday mood, and were wearing sombreros, although out of deference to his position as a respected funeral director Bodie had bought a black one after asking at the shop for a 'sombre sombrero.'

Bodie and Biddle had been calling each other Cisco and Pancho, but the fun element had gone out of the window when it was discovered that Percy Arkwright had been stolen; perhaps he, too, had gone out of the window, and Bodie and his assistant looked out of every window on the ground floor.

Their gaze fell on the Germans splashing around enjoying themselves in the pool. 'Mark my words,' said Bodie, 'that lot will have had something to do with Percy's disappearance. They can be very nasty, they can. Tried to shoot me out of the sky when we were parachuting into Normandy in forty-four. One of these days they will rule Europe, and Britain will be one of their satellite countries. There will be a single currency called the Euromark, and we will all have to drive on the right hand side of the road. And the time will come, sooner than later, when the Berlin Wall will come tumbling down and there will be one huge Germany again. Then they will make us mad by banning good old British roast beef, and they will order mass slaughters. The Krauts will have won the war without firing a bullet, you mark my words.'

Vundatours öbergross courier Helmut Schmartarsch came to the table tennis room from the poolside where he had been organising a game of Deutsches bingo (it is similar to English bingo, but instead of calling out numbers they shout commands to teams of players, and the first team to get themselves into a straight line wins; this was nearly as popular in West Germany as Deutsches Spot the Ball in which they always showed Geoff Hurst's second goal in the World Cup, and the prize was never won because nobody ever put the cross in the net).

'Ah, Herr Schmartarsch,' said Poirot, giving a half bow in greeting. 'It is very good of you to spare the time to see me.'

'Not at all,' said Schmartarsch, clicking his heels together and bowing his head. 'And you are?'

'Poirot,' said Bedsop. 'Hercule Poirot. Ah, yes, I remember it well.'

'Ach so, zer same name as zer famous Belgian detective,' said the blond, immaculately groomed Schmartarsch as he admired himself in the mirror over Bedsop's shoulder.

'I am one and the same,' said Bedsop, clutching in his left hand a cigarette holder like an artist would hold a paint brush, and lightly stroking his jet-black moustache with the forefinger of his right hand.

'Really?' said Schmartarsch, raising his eyebrows. 'I alvays zought zat Herr Poirot existed only in zer novels of Agaza Chriztie.'

'They were based on my detective work,' said Bedsop, confident that the German courier could not have seen through his disguise.

'How can I help you, Herr Poirot?'

'A body is missing,' said Bedsop.

'A dead body?'

'Well it was when last seen,' said Bedsop. 'It was lying here on the table tennis table.'

'Ach, *zat* body,' said Schmartarsch.

'You have seen it?' said Bedsop.

'Ja, it vas in a coffin and proving sehr distressing to my holiday party,' said Schmartarsch. 'Zer was nobody around from zer Britisher's party to ask, and so ve moved it out of sight.'

'Ah,' said Bedsop, excited that he was cracking the case already. 'So you admit kidnapping the body.'

'Certainly not,' said an indignant Schmartarsch. 'We just moved it out of zer vay so zat ve could play our table tennis matches vizout hafing it disturbing our concentration.'

Bedsop did not like the way he said concentration. The connotation of that word made him shudder.

'And where did you place the body?'

'I am not sure that I should tell you zat because I haf no proof that it belongs to you,' said Schmartarsch.

'It does not belong to me but to a client of mine,' said Bedsop. 'Inside the coffin is Percy Arkwright, the deceased husband of my client, Madam Martha Arkwright.'

'But how do I know zat you are not just saying zat?' said Schmartarsch, who was naturally suspicious of a man whose moustache was half hanging off over his top lip and whose accent to his well-trained ear sounded as if it owed more to Birmingham than Belgium.

He turned to leave the room. 'We vill return zer body only to zer rightful owner,' he said. 'But I believe zat you, sir, are an imposter, and I vill haf nuzzink more to do viz you.'

Bedsop silently cursed himself for not having taken more care with his Poirot disguise. He switched back to his Rolf Harris impersonation, and reported to the search party leader, Ivor Bodie.

'The Deutschies have got the coffin, sport,' he said, 'but are refusing to say where it is.'

'What did I tell you,' Bodie said to Biddle. 'I would not trust those Jerries an inch. It was them who tried to shoot down Betty Grable.'

'What are we going to do?' said Biddle.

'Do?' said Bodie, tugging on the rim of his sombrero. 'It's obvious. We're going to get that coffin back. Those Krauts are going to keep it over my dead body.'

A council of war was called, with Bodie addressing a meeting of the men in the Wundatours party while the women comforted the distraught Mrs Arkwright.

'We must get that coffin back before this grows into an international incident,' Bodie said as they sat in the table tennis room. He was having to shout to make himself heard above the Wagnerian choruses belting from the Tannoy by the swimming pool.

'If I may quote the Good Book,' said the Very Reverend Bigger. 'This calls for a bit of the old eye for an eye, tooth for a tooth. If they won't let us have the body back, then we've got to snatch one of them.'

'Great idea, Reverend,' said Bodie.

'Very Reverend,' said Bigger.

'We must kidnap a Kraut,' said Bodie, 'and then we will have something, or rather somebody, to give us strength in negotiations for the return of Percy Arkwright. Any ideas, anyone?'

'Let me go and give one of 'em a Glasgie kiss,' said Bertie MacConway. 'I'll knock the shyte out of him until he tells us where the coffin is.'

'I'd rather us try to use brain before brawn,' said Bodie. 'If it comes to fighting they outnumber us by more than three to one.'

'We need to entice one of them away from their party,' said Sydney Roper, who had reluctantly fought in the last year of the war and blamed the Germans for landing him with Ethel. He had married her on the eve of his call up in the hope that it would get him a cushy domestic posting, but he was still sent in with the invading troops on D-Day. He survived the war, and his reward was that Ethel, seven months up the spout, was waiting for him on his return.

'We could use the Golighty twins to work on them at the double, so to speak,' said Stanley Blunt.

'Och, no,' said MacConway, with painful memories of his first night. 'Save them for if we need anybody to do some torturing.'

'There is,' said Roper, 'one person in our group who could entice Nelson away from his Column. Let's send Sadie Tompkins into the enemy camp. You can bet your jackboots, or her boobs, that she will pull a Kraut and deliver him to wherever we want.'

It was almost unanimously agreed that this was the best idea. There was just one abstention. Farquhar felt that they were going too far, but he was outvoted when he suggested simply asking the Germans to return the coffin to them.

'That's been tried, cobber,' said the Rolf Harris lookalike, getting them in the mood for battle by singing the 'Two Little Boys' hit song.

Sadie put on her skimpiest bikini, and wiggled out to the poolside. She was back within ten minutes with the lusting Helmut Schmartarsch in tow.

Mrs Arkwright, meanwhile, had returned to her room for the first time since the trip to the tannery. She had placed all the trinkets she had purloined during the day on the dressing table before it dawned on her that lying in the middle of the bed was the coffin. The widow prised it open, and there lying with a smile fixed on his face was dear old Percy. Mrs Arkwright kissed him on both cheeks, put the lid back on and then lay down beside the coffin and dropped off into a contented sleep.

Down in the table tennis room, Schmartarsch had been jumped on by the towering Biddle as he followed the beckoning Sadie. He was tied hand and foot and gagged and then propped on the sofa. Then Bodie sent a note to Schmartarsch's deputy, Fritz Pfiefenberger, that read: WE HAVE YOUR COURIER SCHMARTARSCH A PRISONER AND WILL NOT RELEASE HIM UNTIL YOU RETURN OUR COFFIN WITH THE OCCUPANT UNHARMED - THE TRUE BRITS.

It was hand delivered to the poolside by Giorgio, who caused something of a delay in negotiations by misinterpreting the reply. Fritz Pfiefenberger considered it a British jape, and clearly told Giorgio, 'Tell zem it is a gut joke, and ve vould like to show zem ver zer coffin ist and zen buy zem some German beer.'

Giorgio returned to the table tennis room, and told

Bodie: 'German senor, hee says you ees all a joke and they weel not show you coffin until you buy them muchos German beer.'

Bodie was just about to let the Golightly sisters loose on Schmartarsch with their dreaded testicle-stretching torture when Floella burst into the room. 'I tell you my husband ees head forgetting,' she said. 'Ee tell our guests new to put coffin in room Mrs Arkwright where stays.'

Bernie Biddle was sent to check this out, and returned five minutes later with the confirmation that Percy Arkwright and Mrs Arkwright had been reunited in her room.

Profuse apologies were made to Schmartarsch, who said that this all confirmed what Hermann Goering had said about the British: 'They think through their backsides.' He reluctantly agreed that he would not press charges provided, before the holiday was over, he could experience just what the Golightly twins were planning for him.

The incident ended with handshakes all round, and Hercule Poirot returning to entertain them with a selection of Maurice Chevalier's greatest hits.

The truce did not last long. The Brits found they had to wait for the second sitting for their evening meal while the Germans gorged their way through a seven-course feast. It was close to midnight before they sat down to one of Floella's British-inspired specialities: toad in the hole. This sounded appetising to the starving holidaymakers until they discovered it literally was toad in the hole; not sausages, but baked toad.

They made do with biscuits and tea, and a revolt moved a big step further when Pepe revealed that the biscuits would go on the 'hextras' bill.

It was a miserable night for all the British tourists, apart from the Golightly sisters who had at last got Giorgio into their room.

He felt like a chicken about to have its wishbone pulled as the sisters hungrily shared his body. Under their debilitating twin attack, he was unable to satisfy either of them and they took out their disappointment on him by playing finger tennis with his private parts, flicking them back and forth between each other and scoring as if on the Centre Court at Wimbledon.

Giorgio escaped by scrambling out through the toilet window, climbing down a drainpipe and risking a fall to the rocks a hundred feet below. This, he felt, was nothing to the risk he would be taking if he stayed in bed with the Golightly twins. He thought they were *both* psychopathic. But only one of them came into that category, and there was a guest in the hotel who would eventually find out which twin had the real killer instinct.

While Giorgio was climbing down the drainpipe, Bernie Biddle was making an early hours visit to the poolside. He had an armful of Union Jack embossed towels that he placed on each of the loungers as a territorial claim for the morning. He tossed the German towels that had been left on them from the previous evening into the pool.

One thing was for certain: the Brits were not ready to throw in the towel.

Elsbels, Monday

Dear Mum,
Having a nice quiet time, keeping meself to meself and just concentrating on getting a lovely tan. Like I said, I am finished with men for ever. Have visited a pearl factory, a bullfight and have been to a barb-be-que. We are seeing just how the Spaniards live, and the bullfight was a right eye opener. I loved the tight trousers of the toreadors and the big horns. The bulls were big, too.

Lots of love **Sadie** xxxxxxxx

Mrs V. Tompkins,
42 Peabody Mansions,
Cable Street,
Bethnalfields,
London E29,
England.

6

ELSBELS, SUNDAY 4 JUNE 1973

IT had seemed a good idea at the time when Bernie Biddle used his initiative to claim the poolside places, and the Brits stubbornly ignored the wind and the rain as they huddled by the pool in temperatures that dipped to their lowest in Spain since meteorological records began. The pink-going-on-red tans they had acquired since arriving had a layer of blue added as they shivered in the freak icy conditions.

There was no poolside bar service because Giorgio had gone on strike. 'Ees too cold,' he said. 'My hands cannots holds tray. I ham like an Heskimo.' The Golightly twins offered to warm him up but he declined, saying under his breath that he would rather freeze to death in hell.

The Blunts were the warmest of all because they had brought their heavy tweed overcoats with them, while the Very Reverend Francis Bigger kept out the cold by imbibing rum from the Bible. Sydney Roper tried keeping warm by chasing Sadie Tompkins around the pool, a game that ended abruptly when Ethel Roper sort of accidently stuck out a foot and sent her husband tripping into the pool. This did not work out as well as Ethel had hoped because Sydney could not swim and he had to be rescued by Sadie, and the onlookers were treated to a rare case of the victim giving the rescuer the kiss of life. Bodie forecast that one day this sort of scene would become commonplace on television in a series that he predicted would be called, *Bay Witch*.

Bodie kept himself warm by non-stop exercising of his jaws. He talked loudly and without stopping because he was convinced that his mouth would freeze up if he as much as paused. 'There's a revolution coming in television when the Germans take over Europe, you mark my words,' he said. '*Coronation Street*, for instance, will become Coronation Strasse, *The Two Ronnies* will become Der Zwei Rolfs and the BBC will be changed to the DBC... Deutschland Broadcasting Corporation. Our trawlermen will be told they can only catch tadpoles, the Rover Car will become a German shepherd dog, the Krauts will dominate the men's and women's tennis at Vimbledon, and Tottenham will have a German centre-forward, you mark my words...'

But nobody was marking his words. He was talking aloud to himself because everybody was too busy finding ways to beat the cold to listen to him.

Bernie Biddle had found a novel way of keeping himself warm. He was skipping and dancing around the edge of the pool holding one of the sun umbrellas above his head and doing an impersonation of Gene Kelly in *Singin' in the Rain*. Trouble was that he danced more like Old Mother Kelly, and he got his feet in a tangle and went head first into the pool that was as cold as the Arctic because one of the Germans had craftily switched off the heating system. The Golightly sisters helped dry Biddle off by rubbing themselves up against him. This was just beginning to get quite erotic when one of the twins suddenly screamed and slapped an unsuspecting

Bernie around the face.

'What's that for?' said Biddle.

'For biting me,' started Gladys Golightly One.

'Where we wouldn't show our mum,' said Gladys Golightly Two.

Ivor Bodie had to own up that he was the guilty party. His teeth had been chattering so much in the perishing cold that they leapt out and bit one of the Gladys Golightlys on the buttocks.

'I'm very sorry,' explained the gummy Bodie. 'My teeth suddenly had a mind of their own. It's the only decent thing they've got stuck into since I arrived in this lousy place.'

Gladys One removed the teeth from her backside, and they were still chattering with cold, although with a hint of a smile, as she handed them back to Bodie.

'Count yourself lucky that it was you, Granddad,' she started.

'Otherwise we would have given you a right mouthful,' finished her sister.

While a disappointed Biddle dried himself off, the shivering Farquhar made the point that mad dogs and Englishmen were usually expected to go out in the midday sun. Now here they were lying out in what seemed like the middle of a freezer centre, all because they were determined not to let the Germans have the poolside places that they were sensibly avoiding for fear they could catch pneumonia.

Bedsop had appeared as a Jimmy Savile lookalike, and took over the record selections on the Tannoy. 'And now, guys and gals, a little change from Wagner,' he announced. 'Here's our own Forces Sweetheart Vera Lynn singing "The White Cliffs of Dover".' He then further irritated the German guests by playing at full volume a procession of war-linked songs including 'We'll Meet Again', 'Who Do You Think You're Kidding, Mr Hitler', the Colonel Bogey march and the theme from *The Dambusters*.

Among the Hamburg tourists there just happened to be several old German soldiers who had simply obeyed orders during the war, and they quite understandably took great exception to the theme of the records. They retaliated by singing their wartime marching songs and quoting Hitler speeches in loud voices, and it has to be said that quite an unhealthy atmosphere was building up between the two sets of holidaymakers.

It could easily have been calmed down and brought under control by strong management from Pepe, who needed only to switch off the Tannoy. But he thought how wonderful it was to see all his residents enjoying themselves so much, and he joined in the singing with the Germans and also hummed along with the British records while strumming an old Spanish guitar. Floella also got into the spirit of it all by bringing out her castanets and exhibiting some extremely heavy-footed Flamenco dance steps alongside the Germans, several of whom were goosestepping around the hotel lounge. Who was it, Pepe thought, who said that the Germans and the British could not get along?

The now very inebriated Very Reverend Bigger responded to the German goosestepping with a spot of Morris dancing, which just that previous winter he had suggested the English rugby players should introduce at Twickenham in answer to the *Haka* danced with such menace by the New Zealand All Blacks.

Bertie MacConway sent Bigger into a sulk by commenting that Morris dancing was about as frightening to the enemy as *Come Dancing*. 'This is the sort of dance that puts the fear of death into them,' he said, then proceeding to win applause with a display of Scottish sword dancing during which he substituted rolled up towels for the swords. What made it particularly spectacular was that he performed the dance on the diving board so that the Germans could get a full view of his manhood as his kilt swirled in the chill wind. Embarrassingly for MacConway it was so cold that his Big Mac was somewhat shrunk, and when he finally fell off the board into the pool the Germans sarcastically held up scoreboards giving him low Deutschmarks for what was a high tariff dive.

It was the frozen-to-the-bone Farquhar who came up with what he thought was the bright idea of a football match to warm everybody up and also to ease the growing tension between the two rival groups. It proved about as clever a plan as trying to put out a fire by throwing a can of petrol into the flames.

'I know,' Farquhar said through blue lips, 'let's warm ourselves up with a game of football. We can challenge the Hamburgers to an England versus West Germany match.'

'Och, you can count me oot,' said MacConway. 'I'd rather play for the Germans than England.'

Farquhar did not realise just how sensitive people

could be. 'All right,' he said, 'we'll challenge them to a Great Britain versus West Germany match.'

MacConway gave the thumbs up and it was agreed that it would at least give everyone the opportunity to move around and get warm, and so Farquhar went to see his opposite number Helmut Schmartarsch.

The öbergross courier was supervising a session of physical jerks, with the German tourists – all in smart Puma tracksuits and wearing Adidas trainers – leaping around with clockwork precision movements to his shouted commands. Farquhar felt exhausted just watching them, and he self-consciously considered that perhaps he was not cutting the best image for his company or his country as he stood there in his salmon-pink towelling robe, pink nylon swimming trunks, pink rubber swimming hat and showing off a physique that was more Gandhi than Charles Atlas.

'Vas can I do for you, Herr Fokker?' asked Schmartarsch without a break in his sequence of knee bends. 'Vould you like to join vis us on our morning exercise?'

'I was thinking of exercise just a little more robost and competitive,' said Farquhar. 'What would you say to a friendly game of football between our two countries, I mean two parties.'

Schmartarsch came to a sudden halt. 'You really mean it?' he said, his eyes gleaming. 'You mean zat you are prepared to give us the chance to get revenge for 1966?'

Farquhar laughed. Who said the Germans did not have a sense of humour. He looked at the Hamburg tourists going through their exercises, and gauged that their average age was nearer sixty than fifty. Their stamina, he was sure, would be suspect particularly as they had just been pushed through an hour-long spell of exercises. 'Let us kick off on the hotel lawn in twenty minutes,' Farquhar said. 'We will play half an hour each way.'

'Ja, zat ist gut,' said Schmartarsch. 'Ve vill ask Pepe to referee. He vill be neutral.'

'One little thing,' said Farquhar. 'Do you have such a thing as a football?'

'But, of course,' said Schmartarsch. 'Ve alvays take footballs vis us on holiday. After all, everybody on our tour is from Sportsklub Hamburg.'

It would not be the only time when Farquhar thought to himself whether it had been such a bright idea after all.

He returned to the poolside to organise a team. 'Have we any experienced footballers amongst us?' he asked.

MacConway raised a hand. 'I had a trial at Aberdeen once,' he said.

Farquhar was impressed. 'How did you get on?'

'I got three months,' MacConway said. 'Just because I gi'e the referee a Glasgie kiss during a club match. He disallowed one of my goals when a blind man could have seen the ball went intae the net.'

Farquhar made a mental note to warn Pepe not to disallow any goals by the Scot. 'Has anybody else got experience of the game?' he asked.

Sydney Roper, Ivor Bodie, Bernie Biddle, Stanley Blunt, the Jimmy Savile lookalike and, surprisingly, the

Golightly sisters all raised a hand.

'I played on the right wing in my Army days,' said Roper. 'They used to say I played just like Matthews. Unfortunately they didn't mean Stanley but Jesse. That's my little joke, by the way. I was good enough to play for my regiment, but that was nearly thirty years ago.'

'What about your bandaged foot?' said Farquhar.

'Those Krauts can't hurt me any more than that jellyfish did,' said Roper. 'The swelling's gone down, and I think I can still raise enough steam for one or two runs.'

'What about you, Mr Bodie?' asked Farquhar.

'I played for Bury and Gravesend,' said the Funeral Director of the Year. 'This was before the war, of course, and then I was a coach during the war. Well, more of a hearse than a coach really. I was a full-back and could dig any defence out of a hole. Forwards only pass over my dead body. There's a bit of Nobby Stiles about me when I've got my teeth out and they call me the Toothless Tiger.'

'And you, Mr Biddle? What is your position?'

'Quite comfortable, thank you,' said Biddle, 'but I could do with a rise.'

'Don't hold your breath,' said Bodie.'

'I meant your position on the football pitch,' said Farquhar.

'Oh,' said Biddle, who tended to think as slowly as he moved his huge bulk. 'I play at centre-half for the local pub team. I hold the middle together so well that they call me Bernie the Bolt.'

'What about you, Mr Blunt?'

'It's eighteen years since I pulled on a pair of football boots,' he said. 'She who must be obeyed gave my boots away when we got married. She knows nothing about the game, but banned me from playing when she heard it involved me making passes. I used to play a Charlton Heston type of scheming game in midfield.'

'Charlton Heston?' said Farquhar. 'Don't you mean Bobby Charlton?'

'No, it was Charlton Heston,' said Blunt. 'I reminded people of Moses because I was always having to keep taking the tablets. Cramp, y'see. I needed salt tablets to last more than five minutes without seizing up. But I'm ready to make my comeback. There should be no danger of cramp in these freezing conditions.'

'Mr, uh, Sav...'

'Saveloy,' said Bedsop. 'Jimmy Saveloy. I can impersonate any footballer you care to name. Who would you like me to be?'

'Can you manage George Best?' said Roper.

'No problem, Sir Matt,' Bedsop said, becoming George Best in the twinkling of an eye. 'Leave it to me boss.'

Farquhar then turned to the Golightly sisters. 'You are into football, ladies?' he said, with raised eyebrows.

'We used to go to Stamford Bridge every week,' started Gladys Golightly One.

'Until we got banned,' finished Gladys Golightly Two.

'You got banned?' said Farquhar. 'Why?'

'Because we were hooligans,' started Gladys One.

'And beat up the visiting goalkeeper, who wouldn't let go of his ball,' finished Gladys Two.

Farquhar remembered what one of them had done to his private parts, and could quite believe that they were hooligans. 'So what can you do for our team?'

'We can play in goal,' started Gladys One.

'And kick a few Germans between the posts,' finished Gladys Two.

Farquhar selected himself as captain. He had not played since his schooldays, but fancied himself as another Bobby Moore, or was it Roger Moore? He was never quite sure. In actual fact, he played more like Patrick Moore with stars in his eyes and lead in his boots.

The prestige football match between British Wundatours and Der Deutschland Vundatours kicked off at twelve-thirty by which time the rain had stopped, the wind had dropped and the temperature had soared to the mid-nineties. In fact there was hardly a breath of air to be had, and Giorgio refused to serve cold drinks on the touchline because he had again gone on strike. 'Ees too hot,' he said. 'My hands cannots holds tray because it ees burning my feengers. I ham hon fire.' The Golightly twins offered to cool him down but he declined, saying under his breath that he would rather fry in hell.

The Hamburg team came running on to the lawn in matching ventilated Adidas shirts and shorts, and each of them wore lightweight leather Puma football boots. The British team sauntered on to the pitch in an assortment of swimming costumes, beach shorts and, in MacConway's case, a kilt, and they wore sandals, plimsolls and carpet slippers on their feet. They were a man short because the George Best lookalike had not turned up. This was Bedsop taking authenticity to ridiculous lengths.

Pepe, dressed in a referee's black uniform and carrying a whistle, took it all as seriously as the Germans, a team made up of eleven former professional footballers who had been active when Germany last won the World Cup in 1954. In the nineteen years since that triumph they had each put on weight and had lost stamina and speed but not their basic skills and the rather useful ability to pass the ball to a member of their own side – something that Bodie predicted, with some accuracy, would become a lost art in British football.

The match started rather disasterously for the Brits when Ethel Roper and Sadie Tompkins were ordered off in the first minute for fighting each other. Helmut Schmartarsch led the protests, pleading for 'Fraulein' Tompkins to be allowed to stay on. He had been looking forward to showing her his tackle, but Pepe was determined to impose his authority on the match right from the first kick. He had heard all about the disease of British hooliganism and was not going to allow it in any match in which he officiated.

Pepe ordered Mrs Blunt away from the touchline when she started chanting, 'The referee's a bastard,' something she had picked up from watching football on Match of the Day.

The score by half-time was 22-0 to the Germans despite a gallant show in goal by the Golightly sisters who enthusiastically dived on anything that moved. This resulted in them conceding twelve penalties and receiving two indecent proposals from the Hamburg veterans, both of which were accepted.

Ivor Bodie was doing his best to organise the defence, but had the slight handicap of having Mrs Arkwright sweeping up behind him. With his teeth out it had to be said that he did bear a resemblance to the Toothless Tiger Nobby Stiles, but he tackled more like Andy Pandy. At least he kicked the ball forward, which was a basic skill that appeared to have eluded Farquhar, who managed to net a hat-trick of goals. Unfortunately they were all scored in his own net.

Sydney Roper, limping on the right wing, managed one shot at the German goal in the first-half which beat the goalkeeper, but Pepe ruled that the ball had not crossed the goal line after consulting with Floella, who was running the line using a tea towel as a flag.

'You see, Fokker,' said Schmartarsch, 'zat ist vat happens ven you do not haf ein Russian linesman to nod his head on cue. The truth hurts, nein? Now you know vat it vas like for der entire German nation ven zat Geoff Hurst goal was allowed to stand.'

'One day,' predicted Bodie, talking aloud to himself, 'Geoff Hurst will have to buy the ball back from the German who nicked it after the World Cup final, you mark my words...'

Bernie Biddle was playing valiantly in defence and attack, but the fact that he never got above funeral march speed meant that he usually arrived too late to be of any use. He was further slowed down when he had to carry Stanley Blunt on his broad shoulders after he had gone down with cramp after five minutes.

The Very Reverend Francis Bigger was, it had to be

admitted, something of a liabilty and might as well not have been on the pitch. He had claimed before the game that he was very good at making crosses, but had not added that this was with a raised finger and not with a football. He gave the sign of the cross to every German player who ran past him, and marked each of their goals with a prayer of thanksgiving. This meant that he spent most of the game on his knees.

If anything the second half was even more one-sided than the first. MacConway, the one British player who looked as if he could have achieved something if any team-mate had managed to pass the ball to his feet, was ordered off five minutes after half-time for taking a swing at the German goalkeeper, who had felt up his kilt during a goalmouth scramble. 'You won't find the ball up there, Jimmy,' he growled before throwing a punch that laid the goalkeeper flat out.

Pepe had no hesitation in sending him for an early bath (which he enjoyed with Sadie Tompkins), leaving the British team with just seven players including the invalided passenger Blunt and the very hopeless Very Reverend Bigger.

Farquhar tried to rally his team against a German side that did not have a herr out of place. But as he was sold more dummies than Mothercare he was unable to earn the respect of his team-mates who, in fact, tried to negotiate his transfer to the German team during a second-half in which they conceded another twenty-one goals before they at last replied.

The goal was quite spectacular and fairly unique. A German defender hammered a clearance that crashed against the back of Pepe's head, knocking him face first to the floor. The ball bounced into the path of Sydney Roper, who miskicked it so that it ballooned into the air and landed on the head of Blunt, who was being given a fireman's carry by Biddle. He nodded it down into the path of Biddle, who hit the ball with full power just as Pepe was being helped to his feet. The ball cannoned against his head and as he sank back to the ground it went into the opposite side of the goal to which the German goalkeeper was diving.

It was not the greatest goal ever scored, but the dwindling team greeted it as if it were the winner at Wembley. The fact that they had conceded forty-two goals before this consolation effort was not going to be allowed to deny them a proper celebration. They tried to carry Bernie Biddle around the pitch like a trophy, but he was so big that both Blunt and Roper pulled muscles attempting to lift him. Neither of them were able to play for the last five minutes during which the Germans added four more goals to run out winners by forty-six goals to one.

At the final whistle the Germans ran around the pitch taking a salute from their fans. You would have thought they had won the World Cup, and to look at the exhausted, depressed Brits you would have thought they had lost it. 'One day,' said Bodie, 'somebody will say that football is a funny old game. But it's not. It can be very cruel.' But nobody could hear his profound words above the noise of the cheering Germans.

'How do you like zem potatoes, Fokker?' shouted öbergross courier Schmartarsch. 'That vipes out zer defeat at Vembley in zer nineteen sixty-six Vorld Cup final.'

Farquhar tried to think of a telling comeback, and found himself saying: 'But I bet you couldn't beat us in a Eurovision Song Contest.'

'You are on,' said Schmartarsch. 'Same time tomorrow in zer hotel lounge. Your song against ours. Pepe can be a neutral referee. Zis vill give us revenge for zat awful Puppet on ein String.'

Once again Farquhar found himself wondering if he would regret having opened his mouth.

The match had given the British holidaymakers a good appetite despite the defeat, and they went eagerly into the hotel for lunch.

'All that bending down and juggling with balls,' started Gladys Golightly One.

'Has made us very hungry,' finished Gladys Golightly Two.

The unfortunate Farquhar was surrounded by protesting clients when he reported that they would have to wait for the second sitting at four-thirty because the Germans had filled all the tables for their nine-course feast.

For once it was not Evelyn Blunt who was first in with the gripe. 'What sort of a wimp are you, Farque?' said Sydney Roper, spoiling for a fight. He was in a particularly bad mood because he had seen Bertie MacConway coming out of Sadie's room after his early bath with a wide smile on his face and a sparkle in his sporran.

'I did ask for our party to be allowed the first sitting,' said a thoroughly cheesed-off Farquhar. 'But that would have meant having lunch at ten-thirty this morning while you were still digesting your breakfast.'

'Breakfast?' scoffed Mrs Blunt. 'You call cinders on toast breakfast? Tell him, Stanley, that in Guildford we are accustomed to only the finest food and prepared to perfection.'

'Yes, dear,' Stanley had meant to say, but it came out as, 'Stick the toast up your knickers, you horrible old bag.'

Mrs Blunt looked at him open-mouthed, and decided the cramp in his calf had spread to his brain. 'I want my husband fed a proper hot meal immediately,' she said. 'The poor man's brain is suffering from cramp.'

'Why is it, Farque,' asked MacConway, 'that the Germans always get tae have the best food, the best service , the best rooms and the best of everything, while we are treated like paupers?'

'It just might have something to do with the fact,' said Farquhar, 'that they are paying ten times a head more for their holiday. Short of giving the holiday away, we could not have got you out here any cheaper. In this life you get what you pay for.'

Mrs Arkwright, who had left Percy in his room that morning rather than risk him catching cold, reached into her handbag and took out a thick wad of pesetas that had been prepared by her husband just before his untimely death. 'Here you are, Mr Farquhar,' she said. 'Go and give that to the hotel manager, and tell him that from now on *we* want the best of everything.'

Bedsop, resuming his Jimmy Savile impersonation after a less than satisfactory George Best portrayal, placed a record on the turntable, and they all joined in a chorus of 'Money Makes the World Go Round' and then sang 'For She's A Jolly Good Fellow'.

It was while counting his way through the tens of thousands of pesetas that Mrs Arkwright had handed him in a Woolworths paper bag that Farquhar noticed that General Franco's head on the notes looked a little different to usual. On closer inspection he realised with something of a sinking feeling that it was in fact not General Franco but Frank Sinatra peering out at him.

When Farquhar pointed out this little matter to Mrs Arkwright, she shook her head sadly. 'Poor old Percy,' she said. 'He always managed to make a little error in his work. That's why we were never really rich.'

She laughed at a suddenly uncorked memory. 'I remember when he forged thirty thousand poundsworth of fivers, which were just about faultless except that he had put on each note, "The Bonk of England".'

Everybody laughed except Farquhar, Bodie and Biddle. The Wundatours courier remembered that Mrs Arkwright had paid for her holiday in cash, while Bodie was making a mental note to check the bundle of notes that he had put in the funeral parlour safe before leaving on this assignment. He had never seen a £15 note before until Mrs Farquhar had walked in and paid in cash for his and Biddle's trip and the funeral that would follow it.

Mrs Farquhar remembered another time when Percy had been hired to forge a passport for one of the Great

Train Robbers. He was not best pleased when it was discovered on reaching the airport to make his getaway that alongside 'Occuption' Percy had written, 'Train Robber'. Then there was the time, she recalled with a smile and a tear in her eye, when he did a beautiful and absolutely perfect forgery of Winston Churchill's signature on a cheque for twenty thousand pounds. He had copied it from one of Churchill's paintings, and everybody agreed it was impossible to tell it from the original. 'Unfortunately,' she said, 'the fussy bank refused to cash it on the grounds that Churchill had been dead for more than five years.'

It was while Mrs Arkwright was recounting Percy Arkwright's slightly flawed career as a forger that the festering revolt came to a head. The over-gorged Germans came belching past them to take their places by the pool which was now shimmering under a scorching sun. They were followed by Pepe, who closed the dining room door behind him. 'Restaurant ees now clos-ed,' he announced as the starving British contingent queued ready to eat.

'What d'you mean clos-ed?' shouted Farquhar above the roar of anger from his clients. He would find it difficult to turn this negative into a positive.

'All food ees gone,' said Pepe. 'The Hamburg Vundatours peoples verry, verry hungry today after football match and eats up everysing. There ees left only enough for their dinner tonight.'

In the background, Helmut Schmartarsch was laughing so much that tears were streaming down his cheeks as he watched the faces of the Brits. 'Deutschland eats über alles,' he shouted to his party, who laughed merrily as they sank into their loungers alongside the pool after first throwing the Union Jack embossed towels on to the adjoining building site. 'Zer British food ist just like zer Geoff Hurst second goal. Non-existent.'

Bedsop had been roughly pushed away from the record player, and now the Deutschland national anthem was belting out over the Tannoy.

'Don't worry, Jim'll Fix It,' said Bedsop, who disguised himself as Giorgio and spiked the German beer with a powerful laxative. The first shots of the war had been fired.

Meantime, Bertie MacConway had a petrified Pepe squashed by the smorgasbord, with the Golightly twins pulling a leg each. Floella came flying out of her kitchen with a broomhandle, which she stuck up MacConway's kilt, and he let Pepe go as he protected his Big Mac.

The Golightly sisters were trying to make up their mind whether to pull Pepe apart, fight off Floella or ravish the terrified Giorgio when there was a shout of triumph from the Very Reverend Bigger in the kitchen. He had discovered the hidden hoard of German food and drinks.

The giant Bernie Biddle was put on guard duty at the kitchen door while Farquhar at last got the chance to make use of his domestic science degree. Helped by Mrs Roper and Mrs Arkwright, he prepared a sumptuous six-course meal while Mrs Blunt and Miss Tompkins laid the tables without once threatening each other with the cutlery. That old Blitz-type spirit had pulled them all together as a team.

The record player had been reclaimed by the Jimmy Savile lookalike, and he played 'Food Glorious Food' followed by 'Land of Hope and Glory'.

As the Germans relaxed by the pool drinking their spiked beers, they had no idea that the Brits were tucking into their food. Pepe dared not tell them, and Floella was too busy showing Bertie MacConway the arts of Flamenco dancing to bother.

Pepe made a quiet telephone call. He was paying protection money to the local Mafia bosses. Now they were going to have to earn it. The Brits had gone a fridge too far.

That night, twenty-four of the German tourists went down with what became known as Elsbelsitis. Jim had fixed 'em good and proper.

Farquhar led his well-fed troops down to the Union Jack with a song in their hearts. They might have been outplayed on the football pitch, but there was a deep-set determination not to allow the Germans to beat them in the singing stakes.

The ground rules had been agreed with Schmartarsch. They would be allowed just one song each. The words and music had to be original, and the scoring would be done by Pepe, Floella and Giorgio.The judging would be carried out on a three-grade basis: out of ten for artistic impression, out of ten for presentation and, the most vital section, out of twenty for content.

First of all Farquhar had to find his best performer, and he organised a talent contest at the Union Jack to see which of his party could hold a tune. He was pleasantly surprised by the standard although he felt the choice of songs was perhaps a little lacking in imagination. He was the sole judge and jury, and this, in reverse order was his top ten listing, at the end of the contest:

10: Chopin's Funeral March, by Ivor Bodie
Judge's comment: A moving performance, but a comb and paper is not quite the effect we are looking for, beautifully though they were played.

9: I Remember It Well, by the Blunts
Judge's comment: Some nice harmonies, but rather spoiled by Mr Blunt's insistence on singing 'You silly old cow' at the end of each of his lines. Mrs Blunt diagnosed that he is still suffering from a cramped brain.

8: A Christmas Carol, by The Very Reverend Francis Bigger
Judge's comment: Singing such lines as 'While Shepherds washed their socks at night' caused a great deal of merriment, but did not seem quite becoming a man of the cloth. The fact that he held out his cardinal's hat for donations at the end of his performance also counted against him.

7: Bury Me on the Lone Prairie, by Bernie Biddle
Judge's comment: There was not a dry eye in the house at the end of this performance, but it seemed a little morbid, particularly when Mr Biddle mimed digging a grave and then lying in it.

6: The Old Bull and Bush, by Martha Arkwright
Judge's comment: More tears, particularly when Mrs A. sang 'come, come, come and make eyes at me' to her late husband, but the coffin on stage could be just a little off-putting to some in the audience.

5: I've Got You Babe, by the Ropers
Judge's comment: This cover of the Sonny and Cher hit might easily have come out on top if Mrs Roper had not kept putting her hands around her husband's throat when singing the emotive line, 'I've got you, Babe.'

4: Sisters, by Gladys Golightly and Gladys Golightly
Judge's comment: Sung with passion and good harmony, but it was just a little disconcerting to have one sister always singing just two or three words behind the other. It could have got the top vote had they started and finished together.

3: I Belong to Glasgow, by Bertie MacConway
Judge's comment: An inspirational performance spoiled only by Mr MacConway's added line at the end of every chorus: 'I'll gi'e ye the heid, Jimmy.' It was also considered a little unnecessary for him to finish by bowing with his back to the audience and then flipping up his kilt. This could be misinterpreted by the Germans.

2: The Stripper, by Sadie Tompkins
Judge's comment: Visually, the most satisfying performance of all. What a pity Miss Tompkins cannot get within an octave of the right tune.

1: Congratulations, by a Cliff Richard clone
Judge's comment: This captured perfectly what the Eurovision Song Contest should be all about, and to have a Cliff Richard lookalike representing us against the Germans will give us a head start.

Farquhar's final placings were accepted in quite good spirit apart from by Bertie MacConway, who butted him straight between the eyes; oh, and the Golightly twins gave him identical knees in the groin... and Mrs Blunt said she would not talk to him any more, to which Farquhuar was tempted to respond, 'Can I have that in writing, please.'

Now came the difficult task of writing a song for Europe. 'Any ideas?' asked Farquhar, a little more nasally than usual after Sadie Tompkins had kindly placed a plaster over the damage caused to his nose by the unreasonable Mr MacConway.

'I've got a sure winner,' said Bernie Biddle. 'Let's write a song based on Napoleon's defeat by Wellington at Waterloo.'

'I've never heard such twaddle,' said Mrs Blunt. 'Tell him that is a stupid idea, Stanley.'

'Yes, dear,' Stanley meant to say, but it came out as 'Shut your moaning cakehole you daft old cow or you will meet *your* Waterloo.'

Mrs Blunt glared at Farquhar. 'See what you've done to him,' she snapped, 'with your decision to put us in ninth place. It has completely confused him. He has never spoken to me like that before in his life. I shall be suing your company for causing emotional distress.'

Farquhar ignored her, and asked for any more suggestions.

'As Sandie Shaw was so successful with "Puppet On A String",' said Sydney Roper, ''ow about writing a song called Pup On A String, which can be a real tearjerker about a little dog that gets lost?'

'Thank you for that contribution, Mr Roper,' said Farquhar, 'but I don't think we could ask Cliff Richard to perform in bare feet. Any other ideas?'

'What a pity we've no Irish people along with us on the holiday,' said Ethel Roper. 'They can really sing a song.'

'I'm Irish on my mother's father's side,' said Mrs Arkwright. 'I know all the words to "Danny Boy".'

'It's a good thought, ladies, but I don't think the Irish could produce a song that would make any impression in Europe,' said Farquhar. 'It's the English who have the knack. To this day I cannot understand why "Hey, Little Birdie in the Treetop" by Teddy Johnson and Pearl Carr didn't win at our first attempt.'

'What d'ye mean *the English* have the knack, Farque?' said MacConway. 'I'll have ye know that Lulu was our last winner, and she just happens to be as Scottish as bagpipes.'

Farquhar was not going to argue with him in case he resorted to violence again. 'Fair enough,' he said. 'It's the *British* who have the knack. Have you an idea for a theme for this contest?'

'Och, aye,' said MacConway. 'Let's write a song based on Sir Harry Lauder's stirring "Keep Right On tae the End of the Road".'

'But it needs a European feel,' said Farquhar.

'Easy,' said MacConway. 'We'll call it Keep Right On tae the End of the Rue or the Strasse.'

'I still don't think that would be considered innovative enough for this contest,' said Farquhar, quickly adding to keep the peace, 'But a nice try, Mr MacConway. It's just that the rules state quite clearly that the words and the music have to be original. We need something fresh and with a real feel and flavour of Europe.'

'What about Onward European Soldiers?' suggested the Very Reverend Francis Bigger. 'That would sound just right coming from Cliff Richard, and I could accompany him on the tambourine. That would really have the Germans rattled.'

'No, it's still not quite right,' said Farquhar. 'It should be middle of the road but with a bit of rock 'n' roll, some jazz and a pinch of pop and a touch of the classics thrown in. The usual mix for any song that wins in Europe.'

'Where's our grub?' started Gladys Golightly One.

'We're starving,' finished Gladys Golightly Two.

'That's it!' exclaimed Farquhar, with the light of inspiration in his eyes, a spring in his step and a song in his heart. 'We'll write a song about European food. That is sure to have across-the-board appeal.'

Everybody insisted on having an input, and supplied a line of lyrics each that met Farquhar's requirements for a song with a strong European flavour. There are those who will feel that it had too much of a British bias, but there was plenty to appeal to a travelling gourmet.

These were the final words after some careful pruning by Farquhar to make them match a plaintive tune played on the bagpipes by MacConway:

> You go to Brussels for your sprouts
> And get sauerkraut from the Krauts;
> It's the French who give you frogs,
> And the Danes bacon from the hogs.
> From Pisa, of course, you get pizza
> And from Holland all you can eat, sir.
> You go to Hungary for your goulash,
> And to Vienna for schnitzel and mash.
> It's off to Norway for the finest fish,
> And to Ireland for a special stew dish.
> But as Shakespeare has often written
> The best roast beef is in Great Britain.

There was a great sense of achievement when the song was finally finished, the search for the right words helped along by flagons of beer for the men and wine for the women. The Cliff Richard lookalike sang it a dozen times on the pub stage until he knew it off by heart, and all the time MacConway was improving his accompaniment on the bagpipes until the song had developed into a waltz in three-four time, with a bit of reggae tossed into the middle eight to give it a true international sound.

The Golightly sisters, Mrs Arkwright, Ethel Blunt and Sadie Tompkins formed an all-girl backing group and worked on a dance routine they had seen used by the Supremes in support of Diana Ross. Farquhar had a quiet word with Sadie and suggested that it was not really appropriate to remove her clothes while singing in the background. Bodie added a nice rhythmic beat by rattling his teeth like castanets, and the Very Reverend Francis Bigger strummed his coat hanger-size cross like a guitar.

Farquhar, perhaps the puppet of too much alcohol, reckoned that the overall effect was quite stunning. 'I would have to give it maximum points,' he said. 'It could become a classic.'

'What shall we call it?' asked Sadie Tompkins.

'How about Eat These Words?' suggested Bernie Biddle.

But Farquhar dismissed it as too aggressive. 'Any other suggestions?'

'It's such a homely tune,' said the Very Reverend Francis Bigger. 'I think Abode with Me would be quite catchy.'

Farquhar said that he could not abide it because it was a little too twee.

'Let's name that tune Eat Again,' started Gladys Golightly One.

'As We Did Last Summer Cha-Cha-Cha,' finished Gladys Golightly Two.

'Unfortunately there is neither a twist nor a cha-cha-cha rhythm included,' said Farquhar.

'Nae problem,' said MacConway, and then proceeded to play a cha-cha-cha version of 'Scotland the Brave' on his bagpipes.

'Very nice,' lied Farquhar, 'but I don't think we should mess around with what is already a fairly complicated arrangement. What we need is a title that gives it international standing, I was thinking of something like Ode to European Food.'

Farquhar was able to tell straight away by the faces being pulled that his idea had not met with overall approval.

'That's bleedin' odious, Farque,' said Roper.

'A dead loss,' agreed Bodie.

'All right,' said Farquhar, a little peeved. 'I accept that it's not quite right. We need to be inspired by the titles of the great songs that have won the Eurovision Song Contest in the past. I'm thinking of masterpieces like "La La La", which won for Spain in nineteen sixty-eight. Or there was our winning entry the following year, "Boom Bang A Bang".'

He suddenly snapped his fingers. 'I've got it,' he said. 'We'll call it "La La Ode to European Food Bang A Bang".'

The smiling faces surrounding him gave full approval, although the Cliff Richard lookalike quietly considered that his suggestion of 'Bachelor Boy Meets Devil Woman' would have been more commercial.

To give it more of an authentic European Song Contest sound, the backing group sang 'La La, Bang A Bang' at the end of every line. 'That,' said Farquhar after they had rehearsed it a dozen times, 'is just about absolutely perfect. Now let's see how the Germans like them potatoes.'

'But there's no mention of spuds in the song,' said Bernie Biddle.

There was optimistic talk of entering the song in the

actual Eurovision Song Contest on their return, but the great prophet Bodie said they would be wasting their time. 'There's a Swedish group going to enter next year called BABA,' he said. 'They're certain to win it with a song about Paddington Station.'

The Brits left the Union Jack just after midnight on unsteady legs but in happy mood despite a biting wind that reminded them of how their day had started. They sang 'La La Ode to European Food Bang A Bang' on the way back to the hotel until hushed by Farquhar because he did not want their rivals hearing it before the contest. So the Cliff Richard clone switched to a medley of his greatest hits and he led them up the garden path singing "Living Doll" followed by "We're All Going On a Summer Holiday". The Wundatour holidaymakers were on song for Europe, La La, Bang A Bang.

But their high spirits were brought crashing when they found that the door to the Grande Elsbels was bolted. On the front was printed a notice:

> AS FROM MONDAY JUNE 4 1996 THEES DOORS WEEL BE CLOS-ED AT ELEVEN O'CLOCK AND WEEL REMAIN CLOS-ED ALL NIGHTS UNTEEL SEVEN O'CLOCKS IN THE MORNEEINGS. BY ORDER OF EL GRANDE MANAGEMENTO.

Farquhar was absolutely furious. He had just managed to get the real holiday spirit back into his Wundatours party and now it was being sabotaged by that monkey Pepe.

'I'm not standing for this,' he announced to his clients, banging loudly on the doors with two fists.

A window opened on the second floor, and Schmartarsch looked down at them. 'Go avay whoever you are,' he shouted, pretending that he could not make out who they were. 'Ve are trying to sleep. Ve haf ein big contest to vin tomorrow.'

'Tell Pepe to come down and open these doors immediately,' shouted Farquhar.

But his words were wasted on the wind as the German öbergross courier slammed shut his window.

Farquhar banged with both fists on the doors again. This time Schmartarsch responded by opening the window and drenching Farquhar and half his party with a well-aimed pitcher of water. At least, they hoped it was water.

'Which room does Pepe sleep in?' asked Roper, one of those who got drenched. 'I'll throw a brick through his window. It will either wake him or brain him. I don't care which.'

Farquhar shrugged. 'It's somewhere at the back of the hotel,' he said. 'He'll never hear us from there.'

'Well I'm not going to spend a night out here,' said Mrs Blunt. 'I wouldn't even spend a night out in Guildford, and so I certainly wouldn't here in this hell hole. Tell him, Stanley, that I want to go to my bed. Now!'

'Yes dear,' Stanley meant to say, but it came out as, 'Go and sleep in the kennel with the other old dog.'

Mrs Blunt gaped, while behind her the rest of the party tried to repress giggles.

'Did you hear that, Mr Farquhar?' she said. 'I hold you and your company responsible for the change in my husband's personality. The cold night air has made him quite deranged.'

'We're going tae have to break our way in,' said MacConway, feeling the cold beneath his kilt. 'My Big Mac will get pneumonia if we stay out here another minute.'

'We will soon warm you up,' started Gladys Golightly One.

'When we get into our room,' finished Gladys Golightly Two.

'There'll be nae need for that,' said MacConway, recalling the pain of his first-night date with one of the twins. 'That would be stretching things a bit too far.'

They looked around for something heavy with which to barge open the doors.

With the full permission, of course, of Mrs Arkwright, they settled on using the coffin as a battering ram.

'This is best English oak,' said Bodie, as Biddle and Roper and MacConway joined him in taking a corner each. 'It will smash down Spanish doors with ease.'

Well, it wasn't exactly easy. They took four runs at the doors before they finally gave way under the thrusting weight of the coffin.

Pepe was waiting on the other side with a bill for damages. 'Thees,' he said, 'weel be beeg beeg hextras.'

As they carried Percy up to his room, Mrs Arkwright was laughing merrily. 'This,' she said, 'has been one of the most exciting nights of Percy's life.'

Elsbels, Sunday

Dear Mum,
They are trying to rip us off right left and centre, but they're nae getting the better of this Glasgie boy. I have tae tell ye that I think I've found the girl of my dreams. Her name is Sadie, and I hope to persuade her tae come and see us in Glasgie to find out how real people live. Must away noo. We're about tae start World War 111.
Your loving son, **Big Mac**

Mrs J. MacConway,
147 Highlands Road,
Gorbals Way,
Glasgow,
Scotland,
GB.

7

MONDAY, 5 JUNE 1973

WAR broke out on the sixth day of the Wundatours holiday, and it was the British against the Spanish and the Germans. The episode that provoked the conflict followed the mock Eurovision Song Contest that degenerated into something of a riot amid accusations of vote rigging and bribery.

Farquhar was pleasantly surprised at the way his flock had reacted to the late-night shut out by Pepe. It had pulled them closer together and there was a strong team spirit going into the contest. Even Ethel Roper and Sadie Tompkins had called something of a truce, and made do with pulling faces rather than each other's hair. Floella did her best to wreck their good humour with a breakfast that defied description. She surpassed herself with kippers that tasted like cardboard, stone-like kidneys usually seen only on an operating table, and black pudding that could have been used as a doorstop. But there were no complaints, not even from the Blunts, because nobody wanted to rock the boat and upset Floella because she was one of the judges.

In fact the Very Reverend Francis Bigger went just a little bit over the top by blessing the kitchen 'and all who cook in her.' Floella knelt and kissed his hand, while behind them Mrs Arkwright was helping herself to the cutlery.

The first sign that the competition would be fought on bitter terms came when the Germans lodged an official protest over the British introducing Cliff Richard as their contestant. 'It is both unfair and unethical that they should bring in an established star of the Eurovision Song Contest to represent them,' Helmut Schmartarsch told referee Pepe, who nodded his head in agreement and understanding. 'We demand his withdrawal.'

It was quickly written into the rules that professional singers were barred from taking part. Rather than reveal his true identity and so jeopardise his undercover work as a private detective, Bedsop reluctantly dropped out with a curl of his lip, a shake of his hips and a hand pushed through his quiff. 'Congratulations and jubilations,' he said, 'I'm now going off on a summer holiday so no more working for a week or two.'

As he disappeared into the shadows the British were left with the last minute dilemma of who should perform their song. The Very Reverend Francis Bigger made an impassioned plea that he should be allowed to come in as substitute because he had an affinity with Cliff Richard, but he did not help his case by saying that he would perform the entire song on his knees in the style of Al Jolson. Bigger even went so far as to put boot polish on his face to improve the effect, but it was considered that this could cause offence to any Civil Rights Movement supporters among the Germans.

Bertie MacConway said that he could sing while also playing the bagpipes, but after he had given a demonstration it was considered that this could cause offence to any music lovers in the audience.

Mrs Arkwright wondered about singing a duet with

Percy, but it was felt that a coffin on stage might not appeal to any judge who may be just a little squeamish.

Evelyn Blunt, who had made only ten complaints that day as she got caught up in the spirit of togetherness, pointed out that she had once been fourth alto in the Guildford Women Against Sunday Drinking choral society. She boasted that she had the best vibrato in central east Guildford, which greatly impressed Sadie Tompkins who thought that she said vibrator.

Farquhar allowed Mrs Blunt to give a demonstration of her warble, while her husband reluctantly accompanied her with the yodelling technique that he had picked up while on a summer holiday in Switzerland. Their performance sparked off a chorus of wailing and howling from all the cats and dogs in Elsbels, and Farquhar felt that the combination of Mrs Blunt's floorboard-shaking voice and the yodelling of Mr Blunt, still with the knotted handkerchief on his head, was not sufficiently impressive to guarantee high marks from the judges; or even any marks.

He let the Blunts down gently. 'I have never heard anything quite like it in my life before,' he said, 'but I think that it is perhaps just a little too cultural for this contest.'

'We could jazz it up a little with some counterpoint yodelling from Stanley mixed with some rather adventurous contralto scales from me,' Mrs Blunt offered, but Farquhar pointed out that the Blunts were far too good for a competition of this nature. The Blunts, being the Blunts, shared that view.

It was finally agreed that the Golightly sisters would

sing the lead, with Ivor Bodie and Bernie Biddle taking their places in the backing group.

Farquhar's major problem was how to get round the fact that Gladys One sang each line of the song two or three words ahead of her sister, so that it sounded as if they were in an echo chamber. He persuaded Gladys Two that she should mime, and told the backing group to synchronise their movements with Gladys One, but as none of them knew Gladys One from Gladys Two this presented them with something of a predicament. They solved it by asking Gladys One to identify herself and they then chalked a blue cross on the back of her white dress.

Farquhar won the toss and decided to send his group in to sing first. Pepe, as the chief adjudicator, positioned himself in the middle of the front row flanked by his fellow judges Floella and Giorgio, who sat with his back to the stage rather than risk catching the eye of either of the Golightly sisters. To give it all an air of authenticity Pepe held a Polaroid camera that the contestants were told to imagine was a television camera. Schmartarsch acted as compere introducing each of the performers in three different languages.

Although perhaps lacking the stage presence and polish of Cliff Richard, it has to be said that the Golighty sisters performed very well. If there was a slight criticism it was that they la la'd when they should have bang-a-banged, and bang-a-banged when they should have la la'd, but as neither the German listeners in the audience nor the judges had heard the song before they were not aware of this transposition. It was also noted that the under-rehearsed Bernie Biddle was always a move and a step behind the rest of the backing group, while Ivor Bodie was twice parted from his top plate which rather spoiled the overall effect. There was also a slight problem with the middle eight when, instead of the agreed reggae rhythm, MacConway slipped in an improvised Scottish reel, which he accompanied with a nifty piece of footwork that left him pretty breathless for the final chorus. It has to be said that breathless bagpipes are about as effective as guard dogs with laryngitis, but the quick-thinking Bodie came to the rescue by whipping out his comb and paper and picking up the tune. Mrs Arkwright took over as the percussionist, playing the spoons that she had lifted from the kitchen.

It was not quite the finished product that Farqhuar had hoped for, but – as he had pointed out during the dispute over whether the Cliff Richard clone should be allowed to compete – it was the song rather than the singer that was to be judged, and he felt very confident that 'La La Ode to European Food Bang A Bang' was just about unbeatable.

The scores were to be collated and announced after the German song, 'Heil Heil Heil La La La', which was performed by a huge lady from Hamburg, who wore fishnet stockings, high-heeled shoes, a top hat and skimpy satin shorts. She was nearer seventy than sixty and answered to the name of Marlene. Her backing group, all in lederhosen and playing accordions, could have stepped right out of a Munich bierhalle, and their supporters in the audience added to the illusion by sinking huge tankards of froth-headed lager. Those expecting the judges to be neutral were fairly surprised to find Pepe and Floella jigging along with the backing group, slapping their knees and thighs.

The song that Marlene sang sounded to all British ears note-for-note like the old wartime Marlene Dietrich hit song 'Lili Marlene', but when Farquhar protested to Pepe, he shrugged and insisted that as far as he was concerned it was a new song.

Then came the judging, carried out to a background of chanting and jeering by the British and German supporters. The Brits were outnumbered three to one, but held their own thanks to Bedsop who had reappeared as a one-man Liverpool Kop choir. In fact there were those who considered his rendering of 'You'll Never Walk Alone' far superior to the two entries in the competition. But Schmartarsch reminded everybody that it was the song not the singer that was the most important factor, and he then called on the judges to announce their scores.

The first round of the judging was for artistic impression.

For the Golightly Sisters, Floella and Giorgio held up eight-point cards. Pepe awarded seven points.

For Marlene, Floella scored six (she did not approve of fishnet stockings), Giorgio seven points and Pepe nine points (he found fishnet stockings a turn-on).

The score at the end of the first round: Britain 23 points, West Germany 22 points.

Bedsop's Kop choir broke into a premature 'ee aye adio we've won the cup' chant.

The second round scores were for presentation.

For the Golightly sisters, Floella awarded nine points (she loved the backing group, particularly the cleverly delayed footwork of Bernie Biddle), Giorgio scored seven points (he was quite impressed by Bodie's extemporisation on the comb and paper), and Pepe gave six points.

For Marlene, Floella scored five (she did not like the way she kept batting her eyelashes at Pepe), Giorgio four points (he thought that she was making eyes at him) and Pepe nine points (he *knew* that she meant the seductive looks for him).

The score at the end of the second round: Britain 45 points, West Germany 40 points.

This was when the tension turned towards antagonism as Bedsop got carried away and went over the top with his support. 'You've all gone quiet over there,' he shouted at the German supporters, several of whom were fast asleep. Then he let rip with choruses of 'Land of Hope and Glory', but the contest was far from over.

The content was next to be assessed, and that was all important because this rated the song and for that there were sixty points available from the judges.

For the Golightly sisters, Floella awarded fifteen points (she loved the la la, bang-a-bang bit), Giorgio scored sixteen points, and Pepe fourteen points.

For Marlene, Floella scored twenty points (because that was what Pepe told her to score), Giorgio twenty points (because that was what Pepe had ordered him to score or face the sack), and Pepe twenty points (because that was what Herr Schmartarsch paid him to score).

The final result: Great Britain 90 points, West Germany 100 points.

The Golightly sisters were devastated by the result, and demanded a recount.

'Ours was easily the best song, la la,' started Gladys Golightly One.

'And if you do not have a recount we will bang-a-bang a few testicles,' finished Gladys Golightly Two.

But chief adjudicator Pepe, instinctively crossing his legs, insisted that the score would stand.

The judges were pelted with bread rolls and cushions as the Brits took the defeat in something less than a sporting manner. It was not being beaten that concerned them so much as the stench of corruption.

'Eet ees a fair result,' Pepe said, his hip pocket bulging with Deutschmarks. 'We leeson weeth our hears and geev our scores based on the songs not the seengers. The best song weens. That ees the score of the Elsbels jury. Good night, Londres. Gut nacht Hamburg. Buenos noches from Elsbels.'

He was so busy justifying the bent result that he did not feel Mrs Arkwright's well trained hand as it dipped into his pocket and fished out the Deutschmarks.

Farquhar tried hard to lose with grace, but it was difficult when Schmartarsch was jeering in his face while his holiday party goose-stepped around the hotel foyer and lounge singing the German national anthem. Bedsop tried to compete with his one-man Kop, but then got his lines crossed with another Scouse favourite:

comedian Stan Boardman. He started accusing the 'Jeermans' of bombing his chip shop.

'Don't mention the var,' hissed Schmartarsch. 'You vill regret it.'

'It's you who should regret it,' said Farquhar, with a sudden surge of patriotism. 'It's not only his chip shop you bombed. What about the London Blitz?'

'And vat about Dresden?' said Schmartarsch.

'And what about the 1966 World Cup?' said Farquhar.

'And vat about the 1970 World Cup ven ve gave you a two-goal start and still beat der crap out of you?' said Schmartarsch.

As the two couriers glared at each other, Pepe made an announcement that brought the Brits to the brink of open revolt.

'Señors, señoras and señoritas,' he said over the Tannoy, 'thees is a verry himportant hannouncement for Wundatours of Londres clieents. Eet ees weeth beeg regrets of Grande Elsebels hotel managemento that I have to announce that as from today all Wundatours of Londres clieents are bar-red from the restaurant. Thees follows the hooleeganeesm in our keetcheen and restaurant yesterdays when German peeples food was taken and eat-ed. For a leetle hextras, some beescets, toastes and teas weel be serv-ed by the pool after seven o'clocks when the German peeples have come een from sweeming and sunbatheen. Thees ees the end of thees verry verry himportant hannouncement. Have a nieece 'olidays.'

Floella took over the microphone. 'There weel no

more cookings breakfast by either me also.'

The rest of whatever she had to say was drowned by the cheers of the British holidaymakers.

The Very Reverend Francis Bigger, his face still black with boot polish, pleaded with Schmartarsch to get Pepe to change his decision. 'Tell him, my son,' said Bigger in his most reverential tones, 'that no good will come from this, and that the restaurant ban should be lifted immediately for the good of anglo-Spanish and anglo-German relations.'

Schmartarsch gave the worst possible response. 'Schwarzers, zat is blackies, are nicht velcome in zis hotel,' he snarled.

'May your God forgive you,' Bigger said, making the sign of the cross in Schmartarsch's face with two reversed fingers. 'I hoped and prayed that we had bombed the prejudice out of you. Once the bigot always the bigot.'

He then rejoined the British party, singing 'Ol' Man River' in his best Paul Robeson voice as he walked across the hotel reception area.

There was now racial tension in the air to add to the already brittle atmosphere.

It was Sydney Roper who led the revolt. He was particularly tetchy because that morning he had seen Giorgio coming out of Sadie's room wearing a satisfied smile on his face and with the cocky strut of a sated rooster. It seemed everybody was getting the lay – lay being the operative word – of Sadie's bedroom except him. He was paying the hotel bill but receiving none of the services. Sadie had been doing her bit for the team, and thought she had given Giorgio a good enough night to guarantee him awarding maximum marks for their song for Europe. But he needed his job, and, anyway, he had had his fill of the lady called Sadie. She had just about exhausted him, and he needed to recharge his batteries ready for the next influx of 'loco Eengleesh' tourists.

'We're not going to put up with being treated as second-class citizens any longer,' Roper told a harassed Farquhar, who refrained from saying that this is what you get if you pay second-class prices.

Roper looked at his equally cheesed off holiday colleagues. 'I vote that we take over the kitchen and the restaurant and stay there until it's time to go home tomorrow,' he said.

'I'll second that,' started Gladys Golightly One.

'I'll second that,' finished Gladys Golightly Two.

'What we need is the spirit of Drake,' said Stanley Blunt, then staring at the black-faced Very Reverend Francis Bigger before adding, 'Francis, not Charlie.'

'You tell them, Stanley,' said Mrs Blunt. 'We're made of stern stuff in Guildford. We will never kowtow to any foreigners, will we Stanley.'

'No, dear,' Stanley had meant to say, but it came out as, 'Kowtow yourself you old cow.'

'I shall sue this hotel for every peseta they've got,' said Mrs Blunt. 'Their treatment of us has caused my husband severe psychological strain.'

Bertie MacConway was so angry that he was head butting the wall. He felt that his virtuosity on the bagpipes should have clinched victory in the song contest, and now to be banned from the restaurant was, for him, the breaking point. 'Let me gi'e the hotel manager the heid,' he said. 'I'll lay him oot, and make him refund all our holiday money.'

Farquhar, sensing that things were getting just a little out of control, was trying desperately to think of company policy. How could he turn this negative into a positive?

'Here again,' he said, 'is an example of how Wundatours gives its clients the true feel of local customs and traditions. You are sampling the way the Spaniards react in a crisis, and you will return home enriched by the experience.'

Mrs Arkwright, still counting her Deutschmarks, understood exactly what he meant.

'We're sick to death of being trodden on like bloody Spanish grapes,' said Roper. 'Don't give us any more of that company bullshit.'

'We're in the land of bullshit,' said Bernie Biddle. 'Can you imagine how high a mountain you could build from the deposits from all those bulls they breed over here?'

'There will come a time,' said Ivor Bodie, as he and Biddle took Percy for a perambulation around the foyer, 'when bullshit will become a recognised language. Politicians, in particular, will master it and you won't be able to get into the European parliament that will run our country unless you can speak fluent bullshitish, you mark my words.'

Sydney Roper waited for the funereal-paced Bodie and Biddle to return from their lap of the foyer before putting to the vote whether they should take over the kitchen and the restaurant for a second time. It was decided that Mrs Arkwright could have a proxy vote for her husband, but it was not needed because it was unanimously agreed that they should stage the mutiny. Even Farquhar voted in favour when he saw Pepe and Schmartarsch in intimate, whispered conversation that convinced him that the song vote had been rigged.

Roper was just about to lead a raid on the kitchen when the hotel doors swung open and in burst a dozen rugged-looking Spaniards, all of them wearing sharp suits, dark glasses, knuckle-duster rings and with swarthy faces that looked as if they had been quarried out of Basque rock. The bulges in their trousers interested Sadie Tompkins and the Golightly sisters, but they would have been disappointed and concerned to learn that they were weapons of the explosive kind. Pepe's protection squad had arrived.

They took up positions either side of the kitchen and restaurant doors, and stood glaring in the direction of the Wundatours party. Pepe came ambling into the foyer. 'Ah, Señor Farque,' he said, waving an arm in the direction of the heavy brigade, 'let me introduces you to my familee. They protects me when I ees having troubles. Hanybody causes problems, they gets beeg beeg wallopings. Pleese tells thees to your clieents. Have a nieece diaz.'

Roper quickly organised another vote, and it was agreed to postpone the take over of the kitchen. Bertie MacConway and the Stan Boardman lookalike had wanted to take on the Spanish hardmen. 'Let me use some of my punchlines on them,' said Stan. 'I could tell them the one about the motorist who drove into a Spanish garage and asked Pedro the mechanic to check if his indicator lights were working properly. Pedro stood at the rear while the driver turned the indicator switch on. 'Yes, they are...' said Pedro. 'No, they're not. Yes, they are. No, they're not...'

Farquhar advised him that jokes like this could land him in extremely big trouble, not least from his holiday colleagues. He also persuaded MacConway to use his head to think rather than to butt, and accept that he was seriously outnumbered.

The Germans goose-stepped from the pool to the restaurant for their twelve-course banquet, laughing openly at the Brits as they prepared to make the trek down the mountain road to the Union Jack for their last evening in Elsbels.

'Remember,' Pepe announced over the Tannoy, 'Grande Elsbels doors weel be clos-ed at eleven o'clocks. My familee weel be here to geev beeg beeg wallopings to hanybody damaging hotel doors. Have a nieece noches.'

As Farquhar led his beaten but proud troops down the garden path towards the gates, they were singing 'You'll Never Walk Alone'. The one-man Kop choir had made a reappearance.

It took three hours of hard drinking at the Union Jack before what had been something of a defeatist attitude turned to one of defiance. Bangers and mash were washed down with a heavy mixture of beer, wine and spirits, and suddenly the talk was of rebellion and resistance despite the odds stacked against them.

Bertie MacConway, British pint in one hand and Scotch whisky in the other, voiced what many of them were thinking. 'Are we going tae stand by and let a load of Krauts and Dagos dictate tae us?' he said. 'If this was Glasgie on a Saturday night the place would have belonged to me by noo. Let's get in among 'em and gi'e 'em a good Macduffing.'

'There will come a time,' said Bodie, his teeth clattering a military two-step, 'when that sort of language will be considered racist, but on this occasion I agree wholeheartedly with Jock. We did not win the war so that we could be treated like this. The politicians will one day lead us by the nose into Europe and give away our sovereignty, but the average Brit will not stand for it, you mark my words.'

'When you are brought up in Guildford you have strong moral fibre and backbone,' said Mrs Blunt, opening her third bottle of sangria. 'We breed men not mice, isn't that right Stanley?'

'Shut your noise you old battle-axe,' Stanley meant to say, but it came out as, 'Yes, dear... you are so right. We must find a way of fighting back or return home tomorrow with our tails between our legs having let down not only ourselves but our country... and Guildford. I say that the time has come for us to stand up and be counted.'

Mrs Blunt kissed him on the cheek and patted the knotted handkerchief on his head. 'That's my Stanley,' she said. 'The Guildford bulldog.'

‘We’ve got to stand together and fight side by side,’ started Gladys Golightly One.

‘Like brothers and, of course, sisters,’ finished Gladys Golightly Two.

In the far corner of the bar the Very Reverend Francis Bigger, lacing his Bible with a cocktail of brandy and gin, was singing ‘Onward Christian Soldiers’. Mrs Arkwright was sitting alongside Percy, whose coffin was propped upright against the bar. She was paying for all the drinks with Deutschmarks that everybody agreed were a perfect forgery. She had given Percy the credit for them, and he was toasted before every drink. It was his proudest day.

Ethel Blunt and Sadie Tompkins, each into their seventh pina colada, were sitting either side of Sydney holding a hand each and telling him how wonderful he was. They were into a sharing mood while Sydney was more in a fighting mood. ‘I say we go back to the hotel and demolish it,’ he said. ‘They’ve wrecked our holiday. Now let us wreck their hotel.’

‘That’s a good idea,’ said Bernie Biddle, who was now drinking his beer direct from the barrel. ‘Let’s do to them what they do to their poor defenceless bulls. Let’s cut their ears off and stuff ’em up their toreadors.’

The bar resounded with boozy British cheers and applause.

There was nothing in Farquhar’s company manual to prepare him for this, but he had not yet been completely parted from sanity by alcohol. Somehow he had to convey to them that it would be madness to take on both the Germans and the Spanish protection mobsters in violent combat.

He stood on a bar table on unsteady legs and addressed his troops in his best Churchillian tones mixed with a little Shakespeare and with a bit of Elgar and William Blake tossed in for good measure. In the background, Bodie played 'Land of Hope and Glory' on his comb and paper.

'Friends, Romans, countrymen, lend me your lug 'oles,' Farquhar said with as much passion as he could raise through the gallon of beer that he had sunk. 'Once more onto the beach, dear friends, once more. We are proud to come from a land of hope and glory, mother of the freebies where did our feet in ancient time walk up on England's mountain green. Like you, I am ready to fight them on the beaches and in the hills but let me warn you, my fellow citizens, that we stand to get the shyte knocked out of us. We've got to be much more subtle because we are heavily outnumbered. What we need is not violence but tact and finesse. It is not the bomb and the bullet that will win the day but craft and cunning.'

MacConway and Roper, both convinced that violence was the only answer, tried to shout him down. But Farquhar was a man inspired as well as a man intoxicated.

'We would need twenty Sydneys, Berties and Bernies to get the better of them in a violent showdown,' he said. 'But if each of us use our wiles...'

The Golightly twins and Sadie all thought he said willies.

'If each of use our wiles...' he repeated.

The Golightly twins and Sadie struggled to hide their disappointment.

'...we can cause all sorts of major problems. The first thing we must do is get ourselves back into the hotel before they close up for the night. Dear old Percy won't be able to open the doors for us tonight. They will be heavily guarded. On the way back to the hotel we must put our minds to how we can each of us in our own subtle way cause as much disruption as possible but without resorting to violence. I promise you, my brothers and sisters, that as we mount our chariots of fire this will be our finest hour.'

The applause and cheering that greeted Farquhar as he fell off the table was proof that he had won the holidaymakers over.

Then the Stan Boardman lookalike gave them their funniest hour with a procession of Spanish and Jeerman jokes. Just two for the record:

'A Spanish girl called Carmen Santos married a Jew called Abe Cohen. She only agreed to marry him on the understanding that she could continue to follow her religion as a Roman Catholic. "This is not a problem provided you visit the synagogue with me on my Sabbath," he said. After a year of marriage, Carmen went home to her mother in tears, and told her that her weekends spent going to the synagogue and to church had made her so confused that she did not know whether she was Carmen or Cohen.'

'The Jeerman concentration camp commandent ordered his prisoners to gather round for an announcement. "I haf good noos and I haf some bed noos for you," he bellowed. "Furst, der good noos. You are to leaf this kemp! Ja, you vill be free to go. Half of you are to be sent to London, und der other half of you ist to go to Vashington DC. End now for der bad noos. Der top half of you is to go to London, der bottom half to Vashington".'

With jokes like this, Farquhar and his troops were relieved when the time came to stagger back to the Grande Elsbels, timing their return for one minute to eleven. They laughed their way back as they each thought to themselves how they could best contribute to what Farquhar had called Operation Reprisal.

Pepe could not believe it as the Wundatours party made a peaceful entrance just as he was about to bolt them out for the night.

He went to bed content that he had at last found a way to bring the Brits to heel. The protection money was pesetas well spent. 'I have frightened the sheets out of the Breets,' he told Floella.

Pepe's head had hardly hit the pillow before Sadie Tompkins started her personal contribution to Operation Reprisal. During the course of the next four hours she managed to entice a procession of Spanish mobsters to her room with her well-tried formula of a 'wiggle, a giggle and a tiggle.' As she coaxed each one to divest himself of his clothes, her cackling laugh could be heard reverberating around the hotel. She destroyed the confidence of each of them in turn as she laughed at the size of their manhood. It was too muchos for their macho pride, and they skulked deflated and humiliated from her clutches.

Sadie looked forward to giving a full report on the success of her scorning campaign, although she would keep to herself the fact that she was unable to resist one of the protection mob who, well, quite took her breath away. He was the only one who was allowed to swagger away from her room feeling muchos macho.

The Golightly sisters set their sights on Helmut Schmartarsch, the öbergross courier who was seen as the chief instigator of their ban and also the man who cheated them out of victory in the song contest. He was having a nightcap in the bar when they arrived back from the Union Jack, and by a series of glances, dual fluttering of the eyelids and beckoning with the fingers they succeeded in luring him to their room. His fly had been caught in a double web.

With the promise of a wonderful experience to come, they first of all drew from him a full confession that he had paid Pepe to make sure the Hamburg entry won the song contest. 'I hef to keep my clients happy,' he said, with a shrug. 'Zey pay a fortune to come on our holiday and I vill do anyzing to make zem feel everyzing is vunderbar. So you see it vas understandable zat I should see to it zat ve vin the contest even though I hef to say ladies your song and zer vay you sang it vas far superior to our old vartime number vich ve pinched from Marlene Dietrich.'

The Golightly sisters glowed for a while in the warmth of the praise for their performance, and then, so to speak, got down to business.

'Have you ever done it,' started Gladys Golightly One.

'With twins before?' finished Gladys Golightly Two.

'Viz sisters, ja, but nicht viz tvins,' said Schmartarsch, who lay between the twins standing smartly to attention.

He was now about to discover which of the twins was the pyschopath.

Gladys Golightly One had a good suck at what he called his Hamburger. Then it was the turn of Gladys Golightly Two. Or did Two go first and One second?

It was at this juncture that the unfortunate Schmartarsch learned that the pyschopathic twin's derangement manifested itself in the form of cannibalism.

His screams could be heard even above the cackling laughter of Sadie Tompkins six rooms away.

Gladys had bitten for Britain. But was it Gladys One or Gladys Two? Even Gladys Golightly and Gladys Golightly did not know.

Herr Schmartarsch did not hang around to find out. He checked out of the hotel at a rate of knots and returned home to Hamburg wondering how he could explain his sudden circumcision to his wife.

Operation Reprisal had got off to a biting start, and there was still a full day of reprisals to come.

Elsbels, Monday

Dear Pete,
Coming home tomorrow. Hope you're looking after the shop properly and not paying out on too many winners. I'm going to need a holiday after this holiday. The Krauts are up to their usual tricks of nicking the best places by the pool. Have I got a surprise coming for them! I wouldn't bet on them enjoying the rest of their holiday.

Tara, **Sydney**

Peter Watson,
Sydney Roper Betting Shop,
13 Eachway Street,
Hyde Tynings,
London E37,
Blighty.

8

TUESDAY, 6 JUNE 1973

IT did not go unnoticed that the last day of the Wundatours holiday coincided with the twenty-ninth anniversary of the D-Day Landings. This was something special to both Ivor Bodie and Sydney Roper, who had gone into Normandy on the first day of the invasion to drive the Germans back to whence they had come. Now they were involved in another operation, and it was the Germans who were again the enemy in their sozzled sights. Their sabotage tactics started while the Golightly twins and Sadie Tompkins were doing their bit – literally bit, in the case of the sisters – for Operation Reprisal.

In the early hours of the morning they went to work on the pool area. The diving board was lightly brushed with super glue, the pool laced with a blue dye, the loungers peppered with itching powder and the lilos doctored so that they would puncture under any weight.

They then crept into the kitchen while Spanish eyes were on what was happening in Sadie's room and added a few ingredients to the food. Soap was syphoned into the *soup de jour* which was in a saucepan waiting to be heated. A bag of salt was poured into the butter dishes, the mountain of German sausage was liberally sprinkled with curry powder, and the salt cellars were filled with sugar. They put a variety of spices into the porridge, poured prune juice into the coffee percolator, filled the pepper pot with liver salts, added pepper to the jam jars, and injected the potatoes with washing up liquid. By the time they had finished their kitchen manoeuvres there was not a dish, a bottle, a packet or a container that had not been tampered with. Even the kitchen stool was dusted with super glue. They then shook hands and happily retired to their rooms and dropped off into drunken sleeps. It would be quite a few hours later before Bodie realised that his teeth had fallen into the flour, but with an operation of this magnitude there were always going to be minor teething troubles.

Stanley and Evelyn Blunt decided to base their contribution to Operation Reprisal on a game they had once played at the East Central Guildford Painting By Numbers and Embroidery Club Christmas party. This had involved couples having to find each other in the dark by feel and touch, and avoiding the marbles that had been placed on the floor like landmines.

In truth, they had not enjoyed the game at the time because all that hands-on business with people you barely knew was not really their scene; although Stanley secretly enjoyed feeling the proximity of the local postmistress, and Evelyn got quite a thrill out of having the taxidermist's hands exploring her bloomers. He had whispered something about stuffing her, which had given her a good laugh. 'You'll have to wait until I'm dead,' she had said, to which somebody in the darkened room – she could not see who, but it sounded just like Stanley – had cruelly said, 'The way she is in bed she might as well be a corpse.'

While Evelyn stood on a step ladder removing all the light bulbs from the corridors where the Germans were sleeping – and snoring in such unison that it sounded like a Munich rally – Stanley clambered out through a ground floor window and nipped down to the beach and collected hundreds of pebbles. He returned an hour later exhausted but triumphant with enough pebbles in a sack on his back to have pebble-dashed their semi in Guildford.

By then, of course, there were no lights on in the German wing of the hotel and it took him another hour to find his wife, who was slumped beside the stepladder on the floor of the corridor. Stanley thought – or was it hoped? – she had fallen off the ladder and broken her neck, but on close inspection he found that she was into a drunken sleep and competing with the Germans in the snoring stakes. Now this was a contest the Brits could have won, with Evelyn snoring for them. She could have snored for England.

But at least it was a good sound cover for Stanley as he spread layers of pebbles outside the rooms of the German residents. He made quite a bit of noise on his way back to Evelyn as he continually tripped and crashed into the walls after treading on the rolling stone traps that he had set, and he was in such a daze by the time he reached Evelyn that he fell unconscious alongside her. It was the first time they had slept together in years.

The Very Reverend Francis Bigger had been a con man all his adult life, or even taking into account his childhood. He clearly remembered when he was something like five years old pinching two pennies from his old granny's purse and, when confronted, telling her that granddad had taken them. It just happened to be the day of granddad's funeral, and granny, in a flood of tears, insisted they opened up the coffin to make sure that he was properly deceased. Frankie, as he was known then, was relieved to see that somebody had put two pennies over his granddad's eyes and his story was believed. In fact he was given a penny for being so observant.

At the funeral service the vicar had talked with great passion about miracles in the form of pennies from heaven, and it was about then that Frankie decided he would one day become a man of the cloth because the thought of spinning unbelievable tales like that appealed to him. You could tell the biggest whoppers imaginable, but if you were wearing a dog collar the chances were that you would be believed.

He had given careful consideration to how he could best help in making Operation Reprisal a success, and decided to repeat a little ruse that had worked when he was locked up in a borstal during his teenage years following a little misunderstanding over the ownership of some jewellery that he had tried to sell at the local pawn shop. The police were tipped off, and the magistrate decided not to believe his story that he had found the gems at the cemetery while visiting his granddad's grave. He remembered using the phrase, 'It was like pennies from heaven.'

The magistrate was impressed, although pointing out that rare diamonds and pearls could hardly pass as pennies. He seemed prepared to accept his version of events until an interfering police constable told the court that Frankie's fingerprints had been found on the dressing-table from where the jewellery had been swiped. Wear a dog collar or a police uniform, thought young Frankie, and your word was gospel.

He had caused chaos one night at the borstal when he used a length of string to tie all the door handles together. As he prepared to climb out of a window to make his escape the alarm bell had gone off and he laughed so much at the sound of people trying to open their doors that he did not have the strength to get through the window, and he was caught sitting on the floor with tears rolling down his face.

Early that morning in Elsbels he left his room with a ball of string in his hand and headed for the German wing of the hotel. He could not believe how dangerously dark it was considering that they were paying top money for their holiday. As he crept along the corridor his feet suddenly went from under him and he crashed and bashed along the walls as if on a bumpy conveyor belt.

He was making enough noise to waken the dead, but not enough to interrupt the sleep of the Germans, who had gone to bed comatosed by a twelve-course banquet washed down with litres of beer and bottles of schnapps. Francis, or Frankie as he felt at that moment, was amazed that the Germans had gone to the lengths of booby trapping the corridor, obviously to stop just the sort of operation that he was on.

He trod carefully over what seemed a carpet of marbles and tied each of the door handles until all the doors along the corridor had been joined as one.

Satisfied with his work, he was creeping towards the exit when he stumbled over two bodies. He could tell from their loud snoring that they were clearly Germans who had been so drunk they had been unable to make it to their rooms. Bigger decided to have some extra fun by tying their ankles together and felt it would have been worth paying good money to see the state they got into when they tried to get up in a pitch-black corridor rolling in marbles. He flourished a two-fingered sign of the cross over the sleeping couple, and then made his way back to his room to bandage his bleeding feet and bruised ankles.

Bertie MacConway waited until the first light of dawn before slipping out of the hotel. He used the hotel bike – no, not Sadie but an old Raleigh – and rode down to the harbour where he knew fishermen would already be hard at work. Using pesetas given to him by the lovely Mrs Arkwright, he purchased three giant eels, wrapped them around the bar of the bicycle and rode back to the Grande Elsbels. He had been inspired by the legend of the Loch Ness Monster, and had decided to create his own.

Back at the hotel, he fastened the three eels together with a chain of half a dozen black balloons that he had found in the poolside changing room and left over from the Christmas festivities. He lowered his hand-made Elsbels Monster into the pool and watched it glide away, astonished at how blue the pool looked in the hazy early-morning light. His monster, he was convinced, would frighten the shyte out of the Germans.

MacConway then crept into the kitchen, made

himself a sausage sandwich and returned to his room content that he had done his bit for Operation Reprisal.

Martha Arkwright's revenge came in the form of hotel lifting, a type of shoplifting that she had got down to a fine art over the years under Percy's tuition. She crept into the dining room and took all the silver worth taking, and then emptied the lounge of any little trinkets that were left lying around for decoration. There was only one place where her booty could be safely hidden, and she apologised to Percy for making it so cramped for him in the coffin.

'When we get back 'ome,' she told him, 'I will give you the greatest funeral that the East End 'as ever seen. We'll 'ave a carriage drawn by 'orses, Mr Bodie walking ahead in his top 'at, and I'll wear that black dress and coat that I 'arf inched from Oxford Street. It was very clever of you to forge that letter from the Archbishop giving permission for you to be buried at Westminister Abbey. I shall demand a place in Poet's Corner 'cos you once won that *Daily Sketch* Poem of the Year contest with that verse what you nicked from a gravestone in Wanstead.'

Ethel Roper did not want to be left out of things, and after Sydney had returned from whatever he had been doing and dropped off into a deep sleep she slipped quietly down to the kitchen. She started preparing for everybody in the Wundatours party a good old English breakfast, admittedly using German ingredients, that she would personally take to each room on a tray. An army marched on its stomach, and Ethel decided to see to it that the British army were well fed for what was going to be a long and eventful day. She would even give Sadie Tompkins breakfast in bed, although in truth she would rather poison her.

James Bedsop, private investigator, elected to recreate a character from the past for his part in Operation Reprisal. Had the Hamburg holidaymakers not been in their alcohol-induced sleep, they just might have been a little surprised to find a man in a black Mexican trilby, black cape and black mask swinging from balcony to balcony. Zorro was back in action. He stopped off in each room and stole a black box of chocolates from each bedside before getting down to his main business. Using elastic that he had 'borrowed' from Mrs Blunt's impressive range of bloomers on her clothes lines, he tied together the big toes of the occupants of each room. He would choose his moment to set off the fire alarm. Bedsop then returned to his watching-brief assignment. The time was fast approaching when his client would want a comprehensive report, and he needed to be on full alert even though it meant going without sleep for the sixth successive night.

Stuart Farquhar felt that as leader of the party his contribution should be something quite spectacular, but which could not be traced back to him because it would have cost him his job. Mind you, he thought, would that be such a bad thing? After careful deliberation, he decided that his reprisal should be against Pepe and Floella because they had been the ones who had caused so much of the friction by charging exorbitant extras, ruining the meals and acting dishonestly in the song contest. And it was Pepe who had brought things to a head by bringing in the Spanish protection mobsters.

Farquhar remembered a prank that had worked very well during rag week at the University of Great Yarmouth where he had gained his domestic science degree. In fact it had caused such distress for the University Don and his wife that he was sent down for his part in the plot.

He needed help and he enrolled the strong and reliable Bernie Biddle to act as his co-conspirator. From the kitchen they took two plastic buckets of flour, and half filled them with water. They then crept into the chicken run at the back of the hotel and collected loose feathers from the ground, and these were put into the bucket of dough and water along with a mix of white emulsion paint, broken eggs and their shells, lobster and crab shells, well-shaken tomato and brown sauce, porridge, a liberal sprinkling of stagnant water, a litre of motor oil, washing-up liquid, cooking fat, sand, blackcurrant juice, axle grease, and the *pièce de resistance*, a full tin of molasses, shared between the two buckets with some flower blossom thrown in for a colourful finish. This was all stirred together into a gooey mixture that would stick for days to whoever it landed on.

Biddle then got up on tip toe and wedged each bucket above the in and out doors of the staff quarters. Their contents would be automatically dislodged by anybody pushing either door open.

The success of the D-Day Landings was based on everybody knowing what everybody else was doing. Dwight D Eisenhower and Field Marshal Bernard

Montgomery were not exactly the best of pals, but they did share with each other details of their stratagem. Operation Reprisal had no such in-depth planning and preparation and tactics sharing. If only each member of the Wundatours Party had reported what he or she had done to aggravate, tantalise and enrage the Germans and Spaniards. If only.

It started to go wrong when Bernie Biddle decided that he would have a swim before retiring to bed after helping Farquhar prepare his prank. The sun was just starting to peep above the Elsbels mountains and the sky was a striking shade of mauve and gold as Biddle climbed up to the diving board to make what he intended to be a one and a half tuck somersault entry into the shimmering blue water below.

He had just stepped on to the board when he spotted directly beneath him the long, dark shadow of the Elsbels Monster. Biddle let out an involuntary scream, and this was accompanied by a cracking sound like a rifle shot as the board from which he was trying to exit backwards – and to which he was glued – gave way under him.

Biddle almost emptied the pool as he made a splash landing with the board stuck to the soles of his feet. As he kicked himself out of the pool, in fear of his life because of the monster bobbing up and down perilously close to him, he broke the board in half. When he finally got himself upright on the poolside, he was wearing the busted board like a pair of skis and he was a fairly conspicuous royal blue colour from head to toe.

Farquhar heard Biddle's scream and the crack of the board as he prepared to go upstairs to his room. He came running in the direction of the pool on a short cut through the staff quarters, and in a critical moment such as this it was perhaps understandable that he neglected to remember that he and Biddle had just finished putting the goo-packed buckets above the staff doors.

Farquhar took the full load of one of the buckets as he pushed open the door, and he stood frozen statue-like with chicken feathers, egg shells and crustacean sticking from him like a suit from a foundation of glue, oil, washing-up liquid, cooking fat, emulsion, sand, stagnant water, sauce, blackcurrant juice, axle grease and molasses. It has to be said that the flower blossom forming a sort of wreath on his head gave a colourful crowning glory to the whole ensemble.

Despite the glue, he still managed to drop his mouth into a gape as he saw the vision of the royal blue Biddle skiing towards him. He could not, however, get his mouth to move again to shout out a warning to Biddle as he came barging through the door over which the other bucket had been placed.

The contents poured down on to the unfortunate Biddle, culminating with the unkindest cut of all. Bodie's teeth, that had fallen into the flour, were now taking a bite out of his shoulder. Poor Biddle looked as if he had been tarred, feathered, shelled, lobstered, oiled, painted, washed up, chewed and blue-rinsed as he followed Farquhar out into the hotel foyer on his wooden skis.

There was some good news for them. Their movement had been so restricted by the glue cocktail that had been prepared for Pepe and Floella that they were too slow to get to their rooms in time to be treated to breakfast in bed by the well-meaning Ethel Roper.

No such luck for the Blunts. Stanley was first to come out of his deep, uncomfortable sleep in the corridor of the German wing, and he shook his wife awake if only to stop her snoring in his ear. He likened it to the sound of a hippopotamus farting under water. They both stood up and immediately fell down because, so they thought, those awful Germans had tied their ankles together.

It was so dark they could not see to untie themselves, and so they hopped down the corridor together as if in a three-legged race, forgetting the booby traps they had laid for the Hamburg holidaymakers. They stumbled and slipped on the pebbles and bounced from wall to wall. By the time they reached the safety of their own room they were dazed and bruised... and just in time for breakfast.

MacConway was the first to be violently ill after eating the breakfast, which followed on top of the sausage sandwich that he had made for himself. The mix of curry powder, spiced porridge, soapy soup, coffee with prune juice and toast with peppered marmalade was too much for his stomach, and he spent the next four hours on the loo.

Sydney Roper was the last to be served with the breakfast, and by the time he realised just what was happening it was too late to warn his fellow holidaymakers that it should not be eaten at any price. Even Bodie, coming out of a drunken sleep, ate the food. It had slipped his mind how he and Roper had spent half an hour doctoring it.

Within an hour it was a doctor that was wanted by

all those who had eaten the breakfast.

Doctor Hywel Curehugh-Jones was summoned. A Welshman domiciled in Elsbels, he paid a percentage of all his fees to Pepe for any hotel work passed his way. The doctor had been struck off in Glamorgan where he had put all the men in his village on the birth pill.

Dr Jones quickly diagnosed that most of the Wundatours party had legionnaire's disease, with the exception of Farquhar and Biddle who he reckoned had a rare case of molassesitis. He gave them a prescription for turpentine and said they should stick to it.

A call-out charge of five pounds was added to each 'hextras' bill for the doctor's services. He helped himself to breakfast in the kitchen before returning to his surgery where he collapsed. A colleague diagnosed food poisoning.

The Very Reverend Francis Bigger and Zorro at least had the satisfaction of knowing that their traps worked. Bedsop set off the fire alarm at seven o'clock in the morning, and German holidaymakers were shocked out of their sleep by the shrill ringing of an automatic bell.

Throughout their wing of the hotel came the slapping sound of the coming together of feet as the knicker elastic took hold, and this was followed by a loud twanging as it broke. Then came the noise of cracking wood and door handles breaking as they tried to pull open their tied-together doors.

Pepe and Floella were woken by the sudden bedlam, and Giorgio was sent to see what was going on in the wing occupied by the Germans. He went flying head first down their corridor as his feet gave way on the carpet of pebbles. Giorgio finished up by the window at the far end of the darkened corridor. As he pulled himself to his feet with his face to the window he looked down into the pool where he clearly saw the menacing movement of a huge monster, and he fainted back on to the pebble-dashed floor.

Pepe wondered what was the point of paying protection money when he discovered that his 'minders' had departed, apparently all of them hit by a deep depression apart from one who was suffering from exhaustion.

He summoned Farquhar to try to get to the bottom of what had gone on during the night. The moment he saw him he realised that the Germans had obviously started it all by tarring and feathering the poor man. That would explain Herr Schmartarsch's sudden exit in the early hours of the morning. He had been moaning something about the British biting off more than they could chew, but Pepe was able to make little sense of what he was saying because he was walking around the hotel foyer in a crouch as if impersonating Groucho Marx.

'I wants you leave hotel before thees all gets outs of hands,' Pepe said to Farquhar, screwing up his nose as he got a whiff of the stagnant water that had been added to the mix in the buckets. 'I sees and smells what the Germans dos to you, but eet ees own faults for stealing food. They brings eet wis them and eet is for their stomaches not Breetish stomaches.'

Farquhar, chewing on sticky chicken feathers, was in no mood to argue, and agreed that they would leave just as soon as all his party was packed.

As he walked towards the stairs, Floella bustled past him carrying the breakfasts she had prepared for Pepe and herself. 'You breakfast no gets,' she said to Farquhar. 'I geev you beesceets and tea later, but hextras pay you have to. You smells awful bloodys.'

The last thing Farquhar wanted to do was eat. The smell permanently up his large nostrils from the cocktail of food and liquids adorning him was enough to turn him off eating and drinking for life.

He was feeling so sorry for himself as he walked up the first flight of stairs with head bowed that he did not see a wild-eyed Giorgio hurtling down the stairs towards him. Farquhar was knocked backwards into the foyer with Giorgio on top of him.

'There ees monster in pool,' Giorgio shouted. 'Pebbles come up off beach and monster come weeth them. I'm queeting. Goodbyes alls.'

He picked himself up and ran out of the hotel. Pepe, tucking into his breakfast at the reception desk, looked up at Farquhar who was getting to his feet and straightening the wreath of flower blossom on his forehead. 'Take no noteece Giorgio,' he said. 'I tells heem long ago too much laying guests, not enough laying tables weel drives heem craeezy. But he no leesens. How you Eengleesh say – too muchos bang-a-bang. Now he ees loco.'

It was four hours before the last of the Wundatours holidaymakers could be persuaded to leave their toilets, and there was another hour delay while they took turns arguing with Pepe over the 'hextras' bill he handed each of them. He had even charged extra for the use of the hotel towels, the water used for washing, the toilet paper and soap, the duvets on the beds and the 'storage space' of the wardrobes.

'In Guildford, we don't pay extras,' said Mrs Blunt. 'It comes all in at our hotels. Tell him, Stanley, that he will not get a single extra peseta out of us.'

'Stick your pesetas up your hippo-size backside,' he had meant to say but it came out as, 'Yes, dear.' All his holiday-time courage and defiance was deserting him now that the prospect of returning home was looming, and he was retreating back into remote control.

The Blunts had to take time off from arguing over the bill while Stanley helped a blushing Mrs Blunt pull up her bloomers that had dropped to her ankles. She was not to know it, but this was the mark of Zorro. 'I shall sue the shop where I bought these when I return home to Guildford,' she said. 'There is no elastic in them. Make a note, Stanley.'

'Yes dear,' he said, as the man retreated further into the mouse. Mrs Blunt patted him on his handkerchiefed head.

The Very Reverend Francis Bigger threatened to hit Pepe with his cross when he saw his extras bill. 'Good God, man, you expect me to pay this?' he said, his eyes popping. 'I should cocoa. Pray, bring me the manager immediately.'

'I ees the manager,' said Pepe.

'You, my son, could not manage to cross the road on your own,' said Bigger. 'I shall take my complaints about this bill to the very top.'

'You means to El General Franco?' said Pepe, nervously looking at the way Bigger was holding the cross above his head like a sword.

'Verily, verily and thrice verily, much higher than that,' said Bigger. 'I will report Pepe to the Pope unless Pepe peps me up by removing all these extras.'

'I cannot do thees,' said Pepe, wringing his hands in the way he had been taught on his hotel management course. 'Eet is hotel policy to charge hextras for anyseengs that ees use-ed houtside what ees agreed on holeeday package, and you pays bottoms of rock pricees.'

Bigger now held his cross in front of Pepe as if he was trying to ward off Count Dracula. 'Listen, mush,' he said, resorting to the language of his youth, 'you've got as much chance of getting me to pay this money as I have of becoming the Archbishop of Canterbury.'

'What ees thees archbishop who cannot be buried got to do weeth the muchos moneys you owes me?' said a bewildered Pepe.

Bigger shook his head, and put two fingers on Pepe's forehead as if about to make a blessing. 'My son,' he said, 'as God is my judge, you have not got a prayer of my paying you. I suggest you do what the good swan does.'

'Swan?' said Pepe. 'What eees swan got to do with hextras?'

'Well, my son, let me enlighten you,' said Biddle. 'A swan shoves his bill up his arse.'

Pepe could not believe his ears, and now his eyes were having problems as he saw double trouble heading his way in the form of the fuming Golightly sisters.

'If you think we're going to pay all these extras,' started Gladys Golightly One.

'You've got another think coming, la la bang-a-bang,' finished Gladys Golightly Two, who had still not got over the disappointment of losing the song contest.

'This is stretching things too far,' continued Gladys Golightly One.

'And we will stretch your testicles to breaking point if you don't cross the extras off our bill, la la bang-a-bang,' added Gladys Golightly Two,

Pepe quietly tore up their bill, making sure that nobody else could see otherwise they would all want the same treatment. He had heard rumours about one of the twins being a psychopath, and he did not want to risk upsetting her. It was the departing Herr Schmartarsch who had mumbled something about her bite being much worse than her bark.

When Bertie MacConway studied his extras bill he picked up Pepe, turned him upside down and held him by his ankles with his head two feet from the marbled floor. 'Do ye want tae drop the extra charges or me tae drop ye on yer heid?' he asked. Pepe did not feel that there was much room for negotiation, and he quietly screwed up the Scotsman's bill.

Ivor Bodie was angrier than any of them when he studied his extras bill. On top of everything else he had been charged 'coffin parking space'.

'You, sir,' he said to Pepe in his most mournful tones, 'are taking a dead liberty. My highly respected client, Mr Percival Arkwright, was here as part of the holiday package and his widow had paid for full board.'

Pepe shook his head. 'No, only half boards,' he said. 'There were days when he was here in hotels all time using Grande Elsebels faceeleeties. He plays many hours table tennis, and this ees hextras.'

'I am going to report you for discrimination against dead persons,' said Bodie. 'My client is entitled to the same rights as everybody else. Mr Arkwright would die of shock if he could see the size of this bill.'

Bernie Biddle, a picture of royal blue and treacle, was stuck for words when he studied his bill. In fact he was stuck for everything since walking into his own trap. It had given a whole new meaning to bucketing down. 'I can't pay this,' he told Pepe. 'I'm stuck for money just at the moment.'

Pepe tore up a third bill when Sadie Tompkins fluttered her eyelashes and wriggled her bottom at him, but he refused to cut Sydney Roper's bill when his wife tried the same tactics. In fact he doubled the 'hextras'.

It was then that Sydney pointed out to his wife that she had the top of the hotel kitchen stool stuck to the back of her skirt. 'It's not my fault,' she said. 'I couldn't get off the stool after I had prepared this morning's breakfast and so I had to pull the seat off.'

A perspiring Pepe had to keep breaking off from the arguments to rush to the toilet. 'Sometheeng I heats hupsets me,' he explained. 'I must get proper cooks before my wife she keels me.'

'Now you know what it's been like for us the whole flipping holiday,' said Sydney.

It was dear old Mrs Arkwright who ended all the

arguments by handing Pepe a thick wad of Percy's specially prepared pesetas to pay for everybody's hotel extras.

Pepe studiously counted the money, and while they all waited for him to throw it back at Mrs Arkwright his eyes lit up at the sight of Frank Sinatra on the notes where Franco's head should have been. 'Thees is muchos wonderfuls,' he said. 'I ees greatest Frank Seenatra fan een whole of Spain. Muchos muchos muchos gracias.'

He kissed Mrs Arkwright on both cheeks, and walked happily off to the hotel safe singing 'Strangers in the Night'. Then he dashed to the toilet.

Ten minutes later all heads in the foyer turned when a stranger in the day as well as the night arrived at the reception desk to check out. 'Hah,' said Pepe, 'Meester Bedsop. There ees no hextras for you because you never een your room. Has you have a nieece stay?'

'Very impressive, I must say,' said Bedsop through a wide yawn.

It was Bedsop's first appearance on the holiday as himself, and nobody recognised him apart from Farquhar and the client to whom he would soon be making his report. His major problem was trying to keep awake because he had not slept a wink since arriving, and the bags under his eyes were so big that it would almost certainly mean him having to pay excess baggage at the airport.

The feathered Farquhar wafted towards him with an outstretched gluey hand. 'It's so nice to see you again, Mr Bedsop,' he said, automatically dropping into his company jargon. 'I do hope you have had a wonderful Wundatours holiday.'

They shook hands, and then had to go into the men's room together to use hot soapy water to get free of each other. There was, it has to be said, quite a lot of eyebrow raising as they disappeared into the cloakroom hand in hand.

'You wouldn't get that sort of thing happening in Guildford,' said Mrs Blunt. 'You would never hold another man's hand, would you Stanley.'

'I'm sure I would get more response than when holding your hand,' he thought of saying, but it came out as, 'Certainly not, dear.'

Stanley had slipped back into his old policy of 'anything for a quiet wife'.

'Ye only have tae look at them two to see they're a couple of woofters,' said the kilted MacConway. 'It's a wonder they don't wear skirts.'

'I agree with you, my son,' said the Very Reverend Francis Bigger, who was wearing a cassock.

'There will come a day,' said Ivor Bodie, 'when they will have women priests and woofters will be knowlingly ordained by the Archbishop of Canterbury, you mark my words.'

'Then thank God I'm an atheist,' said MacConway, who stopped talking as the door of the men's room swung open and Farquhar emerged with Bedsop on his back in what looked a very compromising position.

'Disgusting!' said Mrs Blunt. 'You would get arrested for that in Guildford. I don't care if they are consenting adults. Stanley, do something.'

'Yes dear,' said Stanley, who was as shocked as his wife by this brazen behaviour.

He straightened the handkerchief on his head, and stood directly in front of Farquhar and his partner. 'Put that man down,' he said. 'You cannot do this sort of thing in a public place.'

'He fell asleep while I was extracting his hand,' explained the courier, his face the colour of the lobster shell on his shoulder.

'I don't wish to know the gory details,' said Stanley. 'I just want to place on record that my wife and I will be complaining to your head office about your behaviour on our return to good old Guildford.'

'Please yourself,' said Farquhar, 'But just remember that it was not me who was pulling his wife's knickers down in the hotel foyer.'

'I was pulling them up,' said Stanley indignantly.

'Well somebody must have dropped them in the first place.'

'They came down automatically,' said Stanley.

'I know what you mean, luv,' said Sadie Tompkins with a cackling laugh, making Stanley blush. 'My knickers have been up and down more times on this holiday than the hotel lift.'

Ethel Roper was disgusted. 'The trouble with that woman,' she said to Sydney, 'is that she's got a speech impediment. She just can't say no.'

Sadie overheard, and flew at Mrs Roper. They rolled over in the foyer tugging at each other's hair. It was Floella who separated them.

'What ees eet weeth you women's mad?' she said.

'You keeps fighteen men overs. They worths eet not. Eef I my ways has I poisons them all.'

'You have managed thees,' said Pepe. 'We all verry verry poisoned.'

Farquhar had found one advantage with his sticky situation. All the passports stuck to his blazer and so he had no worries about losing them.

He organised his party for a final round of tea and biscuits before leaving for the airport.

'Thees,' said Pepe, 'weel be hextras.'

Mrs Arkwright fished out more Sinatra pesetas, and ordered a dozen bottles of champagne. This brought a real bubble to the party, and all the aggravation was forgotten as they turned their last hours at the Grande Elsbels into a good old British knees-up.

Only Bedsop missed it. He was fast asleep.

The lifted spirits of the Wundatours holidaymakers sank when they saw the coach pull up that was to take them to the airport. It was the same bone rattler that had broken down on the mountain road, and seated at the wheel was the familiar figure of Pedro. 'Steek your facking teeps,' he called to them, with a wide insane-looking grin that they found quite disturbing. But they consoled themselves with the thought that in the sun-drenched daylight surely even he would have no trouble getting to the airport on time.

Percy Arkwright was the last to be put aboard the coach, and this time the coffin was laid out on the back seat with Mrs Arkwright sitting proudly alongside her husband, whose clever forgery had settled the bills and brought a champagne sparkle to the end of the holiday.

'You can be very, very proud of yourself, Percy Arkwright,' she said to the coffin. 'Those pesetas of yours worked a real treat.'

She smoothed the trousers of her Puma tracksuit with the palms of her hands, and looked down with satisfaction at her Adidas trainers. Those wealthy Germans, she thought to herself, could easily spare them.

The bright blue Bernie Biddle, with his wooden skis now chopped right down so that it looked as if he was wearing clogs, had needed Bodie's help to get Percy Arkwright's coffin downstairs. First of all Bodie had removed his teeth from Biddle's shoulder and popped them back into his mouth after pulling off the chicken feathers.

He and Biddle could not believe the weight of the coffin. 'Your Percy's put on weight,' he told Mrs Arkwright. 'The holiday has obviously done him the world of good.'

Biddle made one more trip back into the hotel to pick up James Bedsop, who was stretched out asleep across his suitcase. 'I've not taken my eye off her,' Bedsop mumbled in his sleep as Biddle propped him on the front seat. 'She has exhausted me.'

Pepe and Floella stood on the hotel steps to wave off their guests.

'We had a lovely time, thank you,' started Gladys Golightly One.

'Yes, it was a lovely holiday,' finished Gladys Golightly Two.

Everybody nodded their assent, and waved farewell

to Pepe and Floella as if they were leaving old friends. Mrs Blunt had tears in her eyes, and Stanley removed his knotted handkerchief and gently dabbed them.

As the coach shuddered and shook its way out of the grounds of the Grande Elsbels, the Wundatours holidaymakers looked back in open-mouthed wonder at the sight of royal blue Germans running in panic from the area of the pool shouting what sounded like, 'Der Loch Ness Monster.'

Bertie MacConway punched the air in triumph.

The ancient coach had gone a mile up the mountain road from the Grande Elsbels when it coughed, spluttered and gave up the ghost. Percy's extra weight had finished it off. 'Eet ees facking finitoed,' announced the still grinning Pedro. 'Steek your facking teeps.'

Farquhar, spitting feathers, was furious. 'I will see to it that Wundatours never use this coach again,' he said.

'*Nobody* will use this coach again,' said the Very Reverend Francis Bigger. 'It is kaput, clapped out, deceased, done for. This coach is no more. It will be going to the great coach station in the sky. Now, pray, how do we get to the airport?'

'Leave this to me,' said an angry and resolute Bernie Biddle, who went marching off down the mountain road with a look of determination in his eyes, purpose in his stride and a hollow echo from his clogs. He returned twenty minutes later at the wheel of the luxury air conditioned Mercedes-engined coach in which the Germans had arrived at the Grande Elsbels.

Biddle was loudly cheered by his holiday colleagues

as he pulled up in front of the conked-out coach. They quickly transferred their luggage and the coffin and Biddle was just about to drive off when there was a shout from Pedro. 'Facking señor steel here,' he yelled, waving his arms and pointing to his old bus.

Bedsop was still fast asleep, and had been left behind. Biddle carried him to the new coach, and then set off for the airport at what was for him the frighteningly fast speed of twenty-five miles an hour.

They had got to within three miles of the airport when there was the sound of a police siren that got so loud it even woke Bedsop, who thought he was on the wrong coach because he had been dreaming that he was on a broken-down old wreck of a bus.

The driver of the police car signalled for Biddle to pull into the side of the road. He beckoned for everybody to get out and made them stand alongside the coach. Only the dead Percy and the dead tired Bedsop remained on board. 'My couseen Pepe says you steals thees coach from Grande Elsbels,' he said. 'I ees arresting you all and charging you with theeving.'

Farquhar spat feathers in the direction of the police officer. 'We have merely borrowed it,' he said. 'As the official representative of Wundatours I am prepared to pay for the hire of the vehicle.'

'Thees you should have say to Pepe before takeen veeheecle...' said the policeman, who stopped in mid-sentence and looked in disbelief at the sight of El General Franco getting off the bus.

'You imbecile,' Bedsop shouted in fluent Spanish that he had learnt at night school in Clapham. 'These are guests in our country and are kindly giving me a lift to the airport. Return to Elsbels immediately and arrest all those German hooligans who are trying to scare the population with stories of a monster.'

'*Si*, General,' said the police officer, saluting, bowing and scraping as he returned to his car. He drove off in a cloud of dust and embarrassment as the Wundatours holidaymakers applauded Bedsop's uncannily realistic impersonation of the ancient, creaking General Franco.

'I thought it was Frank Sinatra,' said Mrs Arkright.

At the airport, master of disguise Bedsop passed himself off as Dr Kildare when customs officers upset Mrs Arkwright by demanding that Percy's coffin be opened. 'I am the personal physician who signed the death certificate of the deceased,' said Bedsop. 'He died of legionnaire's disease, which I am sure you know has a high contamination risk long after death.'

The customs officers lost all interest in looking inside the coffin, and told the pall bearers Bodie and Biddle to get it into the departure lounge 'verry verry queekly.'

Bedsop then went off into a corner of the terminal building for a confidential conversation with his client.

'Well,' said Ethel Roper, 'what have you got for me? Enough for a divorce and a nice settlement I hope. How many times did he sleep with that old bag?'

'I have a record of every man who entered the room of Miss Tompkins throughout the holiday,' said Bedsop, looking through a full notebook. 'The Wednesday we arrived there was Giorgio, the waiter. On the Thursday there were three Spanish construction workers, Friday Mr MacConway and the toreador from the bullring.

Saturday Herr Schmartarsch, Giorgio again and Pepe, who was dragged out by Floella. Sunday was a busy day: three members of the Hamburg football team, the Very Reverend Francis Bigger, Mr MacConway again, Giorgio again and two Spanish construction workers, and then last night she was visited in turn by all twelve of the Spanish mobsters, and I was unable to hear what was going on in the room for her loud cackling laughter.'

Ethel was dumbstruck. Not a mention of her Sydney.

'Are you sure you didn't miss anybody?' she asked.

Bedsop blushed. 'I must admit that I made one appearance in her room during my Elvis period,' he said. 'I then tried to get in as Rolf Harris, but she said that she had to draw the line somewhere.'

'But what about my husband?' Ethel said. 'Are you telling me that he did not make one attempt to get into her room.'

'That's right,' said Bedsop. 'In fact the only time they as much as touched each other was in the Union Jack on the first night when you spotted them trying to go for a pot in the pool room. That was when you gave Miss Tompkins a good thumping.'

Mrs Roper paid Bedsop his fee of two hundred pounds, and then went off to find her Sydney to give him a big kiss for being faithful.

Bedsop got to him first and collected his two hundred and fifty pounds fee for lying his head off to Mrs Roper.

There were loud cheers from the Wundatours party when they saw Betty Grable coming into land as though attacking the Elsbels runway.

'What a beautiful sight,' said Ivor Bodie, and nobody disagreed.

Captain Horace Winterbottom was greeted like an old friend when he joined them at the bar in the departure lounge, and they regaled him with tales of their wonderful holiday during the seven hours they sat waiting for the old girl to be made airworthy.

'So you all had a wizard time,' said Captain Winterbottom.

'It was quite a carry on,' said Sadie Tompkins with a cackling laugh that could be heard above the thunder of jet engines.

Stuart Farquhar, spitting feathers, nodded his head. 'Yes,' he said, 'it's been another carry on abroad.'

WHATEVER HAPPENED TO...

Sydney and **Ethel Roper** celebrated their golden anniversary in 1994 with a trip to Elsbels aboard Concorde. They had a sea view room at the Grande Elsbels, and reminisced on their first visit to the hotel with the manager **Giorgio**, who married the daughter of hotel owners **Pepe** and **Floella**. They had become millionaires by cashing in on the legend of the Great Monster of Elsbels, even though nobody had set eyes on it since that first appearance in the summer of 1973. Floella had collected the three eels, chopped them up and served them that night to the holidaymakers of Hamburg. She mixed them in with blue cheese to explain away the colour.

Stanley and **Evelyn Blunt** were divorced in 1979 on the grounds of her infidelity with the taxidermist. Stanley settled down with the postmistress, a lady of letters who later became Mayoress of East Guildford. Stanley was banned from accompanying her on official functions because it was considered the knotted handkerchief on his head gave a bad impression. Evelyn was finally stuffed and mounted in 1987.

The **Golightly sisters**, Gladys and Gladys, were both married within a year of the holiday. They met identical twins George and George Witham, one of whom had cannibalistic pyschopathic tendencies. Nobody, including themselves, was quite sure which one, and one terrible night Gladys and George ate each other. The surviving Gladys and George opened a teashop in Devon, and had three sets of identical identical twins.

The Very Reverend **Francis Bigger** became the Very, Very, Very Reverend Canon of Elsbels, preying – sorry, praying – on British tourists, who supported his one-man church with donations in return for him forgiving them for their sins in a confessional box that he had set up alongside the Union Jack public house.

Dear old **Mrs Arkwright** told all her friends on her return that Percy had enjoyed the holiday of a lifetime. She joined her husband in the great forge in the sky in 1984, and had a wonderful funeral, paid for from the proceeds of the silver service she had collected in Elsbels.

Bertie MacConway became the third husband of **Sadie Tompkins**, a marriage that was very happy at first. But then, as they were walking down the aisle, they had the first of many rows because Sadie was making eyes at the best man. Following their divorce, Sadie returned to Elsbels where she had enjoyed the greatest holiday of her life. She settled down with Union Jack landlord Jack Smith after his wife, Jill, ran off with a German öbergross courier called Helmut Schmartarsch.

Ivor Bodie lived long enough to see many of his predictions come true. When he died in 1995 he was given the funeral of funerals, with **Bernie Biddle** – the new director of the Bodie Burial Service – leading the procession in top hat and tails. His skin remained a shade of blue, which blended nicely with the funereal black. A woman priest conducted the service, which Bodie, mark his words, had always said would only happen over his dead body.

James Bedsop had an identity crisis because he adopted a disguise too many, and was locked up in a mental home after claiming that he was Napoleon Hitler.

And **Stuart Farquhar**? He vowed that the summer of 1973 would mark his last tour of duty as a courier. But as recently as the summer of 1996 he was seen leading a group of British tourists around the Costa Packet, saying 'Welcome to Wundatours where everything is wonderful, and *you* are the most wonderful of all.' Yes, he was still carrying on abroad.

DON'T MISS THE OTHER HILARIOUS TITLES IN THIS **CARRY ON** SERIES